At the Gate of All Wonder

Also by Kevin McIlvoy

57 Octaves Below Middle C
(short stories, flash fiction, and prose poems)

The Complete History of New Mexico
(stories)

Hyssop
(novel)

Little Peg
(novel)

The Fifth Station
(novel)

A Waltz
(novel)

at
THE
GATE
of
ALL
WONDER

KEVIN MCILVOY

Tupelo Press
North Adams, Massachusetts

Library of Congress Cataloging-in-Publication Data
Names: McIlvoy, Kevin, 1953– author.
Title: At the gate of all wonder / Kevin McIlvoy.
Description: First edition. | North Adams, Massachusetts :
Tupelo Press, 2018.
Identifiers: LCCN 2018025838 | ISBN 9781946482143
(pbk. original : alk. paper)
Classification: LCC PS3563.C369 A95 2018 | DDC 813/.54--dc23

Cover and text designed and composed in Stempel Garamond,
Lithos Pro and Voluta Pro by Bill Kuch.

First edition: September 2018.

The text of this book was printed at Bookmobile on Rolland Enviro
Book, a 100% post-consumer-waste (PCW) and chlorine-free paper, and
the book was manufactured entirely using renewables-derived electricity
from Minnesota's Odell Wind Farm and North Star Solar Project.

Ancient
Forest
Friendly™

Tupelo Press
P.O. Box 1767, North Adams, Massachusetts 01247
(413) 664-9611 / editor@tupelopress.org / www.tupelopress.org

Tupelo Press is an award-winning independent literary press that
publishes fine fiction, non-fiction, and poetry in books that are a joy
to hold as well as read. Tupelo Press is a registered 501(c)(3) non-profit
organization, and we rely on public support to carry out our mission
of publishing extraordinary work that may be outside the realm of the
large commercial publishers. Financial donations are welcome and are
tax deductible.

To BH and JS, gifts of sunlight

AT THE GATE OF ALL WONDER

October 17, 2016

I have self-delivered now, living in almost absolute isolation for twelve years. I acknowledge that these conditions have caused old friends and family to call me "eccentric," though "incautious" is the better word choice.

I am an incautious eighty-year-old as I write about my long-ago adventures with the two children, Betty and Janet, whom I once called "the one" and "the other." I write for them and for all wanderers in the secret sonic gardens. These pages, which comprise my dark memory album of October 2003 through September 2004, are my Grimm story of white pebbles and breadcrumbs and windows of clear sugar. They are my private-journal tall tale, my witch-fire, my listening tracks, my deflections. They are my field notes, my after-the-fact added commentary, my fabular confessions.

October 2–8, 2003

"Your heads are so full of water," I said to my two little things, eight and six years old.

They remember. I know they do.

We were hovering over the dark and pooling creek a few yards from our campsite. The thunder sounded as if that spiraling liquid mirror was its source.

"Pea!" called out the one, swaying in order to swirl in that mirror. My name, Samantha Peabody, a perfectly acceptable name, was not good enough for this one.

"Pea!" she called again.

The other swirl-swayed. The other always imitated her older sister. She said, "We're lost!" which she had been saying all morning. Her delight about being lost was only a slight re-keying of her sister's delight and worry.

I lost child-things. The grayparents agreed in advance that I would lose the children for a week each month. One can agree to be lost even if it is pretend-lost and even if it is on schedule, and still there is fear. With the use of escalating fear inside disorienting pleasure, one can hold the attention of suggestible fledgling things.

These were my lost things, these two.

I was there making a face on the face where their faces were. I swayed over them and I made chewing noises. Since I could pretend-chew on the swirling bills of their new red baseball caps, I did so with the maternal instinct of species in which the natal season is cannibal snack-time. Like a praying mantis, I chewed at the ears and necks of the two things reflected on the surface of the water as though they were my own upon which to feast. It was a scary pretend game that they enjoyed. Their graymother Carla was seventy-three years old at that time, and she was not particularly interested in such games.

I made a living from the children. It would not be inaccurate for me to say that such children were my primary diet.

I took female children between the age of five and nine into the Dreaming Pines Campground of the Pisgah National Forest where I offered them an initiation into the unique soundscape of Upper Desnos Creek.

"Lose Your Female Children" was the motto of SONIC AD-VENTURES WITH SAMANTHA PEABODY, my enterprise exclusively serving graymothers. The graymothers signed up their little things for a period that covered a sonic adventure for one week of every month. Tuition was extremely expensive. The adventures separated grayparents and things for eighty-four days a year, giving relief to the grandparent-age women who had irrationally welcomed full-time mothering roles profoundly beyond their tolerance capacities. What male

in the United States in the twenty-first century could ever take up this lucrative enterprise and not have the very idea hunted down and killed? I, a sixty-seven-year-old female, on the other hand, could corner this market, could make a glass ceiling males could not break. My conscripted things were, of course, in the kinds of private and alternative schools in which the absent days could be readily excused or could even be assigned life-skills academic credit.

The contract fee was non-negotiable; the full fee, paid in advance, was non-refundable; if the thing or the grayparent of the thing failed Samantha Peabody's expectations in the first week or on any of the subsequent adventure weeks, the contract was void, the full fee mine to keep.

I pre-emptively rejected the parents and the things who had doubts of any kind about me; I rejected the ones who gave me doubts about them. I did not sign repeat contracts with customers who had concerns about my use of uncensored "adult language."

Before I had begun my Sonic Adventures business I had lost many, many things that I would never find again. I had learned calculated self-protection.

Over the years I had hired forceful female executives of accounting agencies to assist me. Influential female doctors and therapists and moneyed female ministers endorsed me. Powerful female attorneys prevented me from risk of liability. Elderly businesswomen, psychiatrists, psychologists, ministers, and doctors made up a considerable percentage of my customer base, including the subspecies of attorney who was adoptive graymother to the one and the other.

*

The first week in October all the forest crown-limbs clattered and fallen pine needles broomed the surface roots. We could hear one crisp leaf falling a hundred and fifty feet through skeletal tulip tree branches and one bit of loosed bluff-stone grumbling and crunching against a rocky part of the path behind us. The ashen clouds were darkening, as I had wished: a threatening hour to be lost. I had explained to the two child-things that this was the time of the orographic phenomena of thunder without rain.

For their edification, I talked up to children. I talked down to them only rarely, aware that I was doing so for my personal satisfaction.

When the other insisted, and the one supported her in her questioning the word "orographic," I explained that I knew their mother quite well, and, I said, "You know how it feels to hear a cruel word with no words of mercy following?" I said, "You know how it sounds when your mother calls you 'Stupid Thing' only for the sake of being right about you? This is an orographic phenomenon."

They nodded yes.

Rain, which is more cruel by far than thunder, does not sound as unkind. Thunder is the mean master's mean servant. Thunder is the warning you doubt, though you cannot afford the doubt.

"Have you heard?" I asked. There is no question more important, and so I asked it often.

I did not allow the things to take field notes; I trained them in the attentiveness that required they clear and refresh and newly sensitize their hearing. They had the materials I provided for live-specimen collection; each had a Coddington hand-lens magnifier for examining barely visible and invisible creatures making sound. They had binoculars and a strict set of rules for ignoring them while always carrying them. They had Samantha Peabody, exacting bioacoustician, unrelenting teacher, method-ological, indifferent to their puny defenses against learning.

We had enjoyed playing before the mirroring creek. They had let their guards down.

"Put your heads in," I said.

The idea instantly appealed to the other. It did not appeal to the one, and, needless to say, that influenced the other.

"You will not hear unless your ears go in for no less than three seconds," I said. "At this particular location the creek is not cold — the water might seem cold at first but it is not," and I put my hand in the water, and very secretly felt it turn blue.

I had made approximations. I said, "In twelve seconds there will be thunder. I can allow you six seconds to deliberate."

They bowed over the surface. They breathed, blew. The bills of their caps lipped their reflections.

I took their heads in my hands and, without forcing, assisted the things into the water up to their shoulders.

I pulsed my fingers on their slender necks.

Fa.

So.

La.

Me. I was not at all surprised that their caps were unscrewed from their heads by the flowing water, which carried them away.

Fa. I pulled them out and pressed their heads against my chest.

The soaked things shivered; their girl-cherry faces had turned ghosty, their eyes had brightened with fear-joy.

"Have you heard?" I asked. I knew they had: the dark monstering, the dark deviling, the whispering in-breath echo of the thunder's out-breath — all of this inside the sunlight on the water.

They thumpingly hugged me, muttered and whimpered against me. I listened. I heard.

They sounded like the river they had sounded.

At the camp I gave them dry towels. I explained that we could not retrieve their caps. I made it clear they could not yet enter the tent.

"Pea?" said the one, "that isn't fair."

I did not answer.

"Pea?" said the one. "Pea?" And that made the other ask.

"I do not hear whimpering," I said. "Children's whimpering, which occurs almost exclusively in subvocal expression, is not audible to Samantha Peabody."

They were hugging me still. Dampening my chest.

"Some music when we go in there?" asked the one, and "when can we go in?" And the other interrupted, "When? When?" and the one asked, "Will there be some music?"

"We'll see," I said. "You will drip not at all in our tent? You will groom yourselves? You will neaten your assigned tent space? You will not request feeding until after naptime?"

The rules had all been meticulously explained in the contract. In the presence of their graymother Carla, we had reviewed every rule. I'd suspected Carla would not reinforce my rules.

*

(When you feel you cannot possibly love her — I know you do love Carla and I know you have not abandoned her all these years later — I ask you to remember the love that caused this older woman to adopt you as babies and welcome you into her life so late, so unselfishly.)

*

I adjusted their towel turbans, pulled them down over their ears, their brows. The other made a feeble moaning that certain spring peepers make when they are still under the mud but are restlessly practicing. Inside the tent I helped them draw their sleeping bags over their bodies. I frowned at their shivering, grubbing sounds. Chagrined, they attached themselves to my legs. I could have thought of them as appealing things if I ever felt such weakness.

The one said, "The water was cold."

The other said, "You could hear how cold it was."

"I liked it," said the one.

"All right, then," I said and brought out my harp sling with the seven major keys of Hohner Special 20s.

There is a kind of self-deliverance that involves killing yourself, and there is a kind that involves retreating from the company of others, or that involves retreating from yourself into the place where all sound reaches you through the chambers you have abandoned. There is a kind that involves never traveling back out through those chambers again. The possibility of all the choices is evident in one's own sounds. Put the lowest note of the lowest octave to your mouth. Blow. Draw. Pull down that note you play on the draw. You are asking yourself the question, *Have you heard?*

Huge, my harmonica teacher, taught me you get only ugly if you bend a note toward beauty, you get beauty only if you bend the same note toward ugly. I bent the turnaround note for them, which caused a smile on the one thing, a smile on the other.

They sang "Rye Whiskey" with me after I explained that we could sing this song if we were lost, that ordinarily young things should neither sing this very adult song as nestlings nor as fledglings, but that it was permissible if we were lost and would never be found.

"When you will never be found," I said, "when you are lost — you will be lost, that is a certainty — and you remember that I have told you not to worry, to take your naps, and I give you directions to a safe place that will always be safe no matter what, and then I go to get help — that is a good time for music." I could not imagine that they would ever grow to be older things with mates they had not warned off, had not used, abandoned, killed, eaten.

I said that one was assigned mandolin-like sounds and the other must draw the bow across an imaginary fiddle, and together they must sing this part by yi-yi-ing, "Sometimes I drink whiskey — sometimes I drink wi-yi-yi-yiiiiiine."

I did not allow laughter, for "Rye Whiskey" was a sad song of exulting self-disgust.

Instead, I asked that they close their eyes. Close them. Do as I say. "Sing after me," I said. "If the women don't kill me I'll live til I di-yi-yi-yiiiii-ii-ii-iiiii."

It was about fifteen minutes past one o'clock, a dim afternoon. We were being drummed on and howled at, our tent skin tatted by tree seeds. The nutting trees were in a mast season; they were flinging down their fruit in superabundant pleasure; barking and spitting sounds came from red squirrels almost mad with gluttony; somewhere nearby, white-tailed bucks were scraping velvet growth from their antlers in skreakings something like the sound of nails being pulled from wet timber. I sang, "'Rye whiskey, rye whiskey, rye whiskey,' I cry, 'if I don't get rye whiskey I surely will di-yi-yi-yiiiiiiii!'" Eyes closed, they had stopped plunking and bowing, and now they faintly sang after me and fought only a little the intimations of sleep and lostness.

I made a wish that the remaining family and friends I had left would give up on me once and for all.

I practiced my split four-note chords in order to attain a

Hammond-organ-drunken-accordion-hummingbird effect. Around this time of year, the young hummingbirds were leaving the woods in groups; the males and then groups of females had left in September, and, now, the young. Birders name the group "a glittering of hummingbirds" and "a bouquet of hummingbirds," and "a hover," "a shimmer." I like best when they are referred to as "a tune" of hummingbirds.

While the two things napped, I tried more vibrato, put the harp deeper into my mouth. Quieter and quieter, as Huge had instructed, I pulled the notes into my windpipe where I could choke them, and down to my solar plexus where I could choke them harder.

His name was actually Eugene Meadows. He told me that in the service people had changed it from Eugene to Eug, which they pronounced "Yewg." And that name was shortened yet again to "Huge." He had been Huge since he was twenty-six. A tough teacher. At exactly the time you were least and most ready, he would back up to something you should have learned, or he would move on to something you could learn immediately and properly learn in the far distant future. He taught me for seven years. My education mentors — at Warren Wilson College, University of Aberdeen, and Institutes of Acoustics at University of York — could not match the wisdom he offered.

In the tent, late afternoon, pretending to be lost in the forest with these two, I missed Huge, who was ninety-one years old when he'd died a month before my sonic adventure with them. I had gone to his home to play really awfully for him (his wife Biz asked me) on his last days, to play and sing "She Could Work that Stuff," which was a ribald tune he liked.

When I finished, I said, "You understand? — I'm going to miss you for awhile, Huge." He couldn't answer. He was at the end.

"I'm not exactly sorry to be more alone," I said, "but for a while I'm going to miss you bad." It was in that season when you can hear the difference in how the crickets chirp on the warm days from the cold days. He had died while I was there. And quiet came, for which I was thankful.

I knocked spit out of the middle octave of the harp. I remembered: the freezing, the thawing, the cycles of quiet in which his body's sounds lifted out of him the way small stones surface when they are lifted by frost and imperceptibly fall away from their warming cradles into cool air and sunlight.

I asked the things, "Have you heard?" but they were asleep, towel-turbans ajar, faces twitching.

*

In that area of the Pisgah where there are black bears actively hunting in October, one must store food in tightly sealed containers that one must keep far from the campsite. Stowing food high in a tree is advisable, even in a mast season in which there is a hundredfold more food than all the nut-hunting woodland creatures can possibly gather. A mast season is the strategy of trees that have detected a critical point of forest stress. A stand of trees is an intelligence; it retreats, advances, conserves, produces, and overproduces according to the sempiternal impulses of relenting and surviving and relenting, about which human beings have become ignorant.

We ate our morning and late afternoon meal — I did not believe in a dinner hour for adventurers — about eight-hundred yards downriver from our campsite. We washed our food kits there. We did not spill upon ourselves. We did not permit particles of food or oily smears upon our faces, hands, and arms. We sealed our remaining food and drink inside an odor-proof liner sealed inside a canister which we hung on one of the park's bear cables. Any respectable bear could climb to the cable and eventually figure out our system. But the bear would have to prefer our food over the feast the woods provided.

We did not eat preferable food.

After their naptime, as the two things and I partook, they talked. They were discussing their graymother and her "problem." She seemed similar to and different from the person I knew: a divorce attorney, thirty-three years in private practice, prominent in Buncombe County because of her success rate, and infamous for her viciousness.

I found her repugnant.

I found her beneficial.

That was what I told the two things, explaining the natural phenomenon of commensalism: Samantha Peabody was an organism that benefitted from their graymother, and their graymother was not adversely affected by the association; on the other hand, the two things benefitted from Samantha Peabody, but Samantha Peabody was not affected by the two things.

*

(At that time, I believed — falsely believed — that I could maintain impersonal observation of you. Do you remember how determined I was to study you as specimens instead of loving you?

I remember.)

＊

Clearly, they were having trouble adjusting to Carla's newest boyfriend, Warren, whom they referred to as War.

Three weeks earlier, I had encountered War and Carla at the grocery store checkout. Without compunction, I had told them that they threw off sparks of happiness, the kind of lie that an impaired couple in their seventies might need to hear. My cart parked right behind them, I had listened to them making accommodating vocalizations. I took advantage of the proximity, and I privately observed that only upon very close examination could one distinguish between Warren's rectum sounds and his mouthpart sounds. He was a Chief District Court Judge.

The other said, "She's un-nicer," referring to her graymother.

The one said, "Mmmmhmmm."

The other said, "War's like everywhere."

The one said, "War goes to church sometimes."

"But then —" said the other, and the one said, "—he's everywhere."

And the one said, "Have you heard?" She bowed her head slightly as a person must do who bends to the world's sonic current.

"I heard," said the younger sister.

What they described to each other were mating sounds. Or,

more likely, fighting sounds. When I noted that the male cry was probably longer than the female cry and of more emphatic pitch than their description indicated, we practiced the sounds together in order to reinforce habits of calibrating.

This practice was enjoyable.

They talked more about Warren and their graymother's fervid episodes. I did not prevent adventurers from talking during our mealtimes, since their noises constituted a warning to harmful creatures who might wish to approach: We are human children in your woods. Our excruciatingly inane talk will repel you more the closer you come.

We washed our hands and arms and faces in the creek. "Cold," said the one. "Cold," said the other. "Quite cold," said the one, mocking Samantha Peabody who was fascinated by coldness in all forms. Already, they were learning attentiveness.

As we pulleyed our food up toward the cable, I asked them to give me their conclusions about the sounds.

They required my assistance to help them understand. And so I explained that in certain cases the alpha female spider, without regard for her young, will choose fuck-buddies and will forage with them and fight over food sources and will lose limbs to them but will regenerate the limbs and will fuck with and fight with the strong male until almost every limb is torn off her, but will grow strong limbs, stronger in some cases than the first limbs. I explained that eventually she will wrap the male in a swathing band as she is fucking him, and will fit the swathing band tightly while whispering kindnesses to the silken package, and these kindnesses, which come from the abdomen, are called *spinto*. I explained that we do not really hear these sounds that come from her while she is eating his creamy contents in thousands upon thousands of draining bites.

"We don't hear them?" the other asked.

"They are imagined sounds," I answered. "You must not discount them from the sonic dimension of the present moment."

The older gave me the look, and the younger a similar look.

I explained: "We hear a spoon knock against the sides of the cup when we are stirring something; and we believe we hear the liquid in the cup burbling. We do *not* hear the liquid in the cup burbling. We definitely do not hear that with our ears. But the spoon has been stirred by the burbling we do not hear. And we have been stirred by the spoon."

I wanted to say that spoon by spoon we experience the system, the totum, and the quantum of a boundless sonic contour. I am, often, quite often, tempted to plagiarize Pierre Teilhard de Chardin since I believe in the concept of the noosphere as others believe in God, and I own no bibles more important than these seven: Pierre Teilhard de Chardin's *The Phenomenon of Man*; R. Murray Schafer's *The Soundscape*; Walter Benjamin's *Illuminations*; Ralph Waldo Emerson's *Nature*; F. Schuyler Mathews's *Field Book of Wild Birds and Their Music*; Jean Giono's *The Man Who Planted Trees*; and *The Autobiography of Maria Martin, Watercolor Painter for John James Audubon*. I hope that at the moment in time when they are perusing these pages the two will consider this list as proper citation. I believe that inadequate in-text citation is undignified.

*

This was my final expedition before I exiled myself absolutely.

I'm aware that the pages into which I am spilling my remember-ings are pointless: I was a forgetful and forgettable person. I was an unintelligent and unintelligible teacher, an altered instrument of refringence. The writing in this album, which I cannot stop — I wish I could stop — I often wish I could — the writing started when they sent me a letter.

I share a mailbox with Drummer Wilren, my mycologist nun-musician ex-smuggler escaped-convict lover at Mansour Cove over a mile of difficult trail away.

My self-deliverance has not been perfect. I have retreated from the world, but I re-enter it here in this album. I retrieve from the darknesses the shining dark resonances of that year.

In early March and in September I have sexual contact, nocturnal and diurnal, with Drummer. She was named for her great-great grandmother who was a woods-to-woods itinerant saleswoman (a "drummer," hill folk called such a person) of "Woman's Goods & Formulas" from about 1896 to 1938.

A year ago, Drummer brought me a long, warm and loving letter from the two.

I have not answered.

I have discerned that the first half is in the voice of the one; the second half, the other.

They warn that they are coming to visit me on my eightieth birthday, October 17, 2016.

The one is twenty-one now. The other is nineteen. They ended their letter in this manner:

Have you heard?
Betty
Have you heard?
Janet

We hiked up-creek between Little Char Knob and Jacob Mountain where I taught the children about the raccoon and heron vocalizations we heard at the creek bank. I identified their tracks and the substrate-level evidence of individual animals and animal packs moving to and from sources of food and community. Trappers learned these paths, and poachers.

We had stopped too long in order to hear leaves, twigs, berries, and wormed-through chips of bark hit the water. With only an hour of daylight left and the sky swelling with rain, we were hiking down at a pace. Our reception of sound was affected by the micropulses of moist air in the canopy and the understory. I explained that the rain sound we thought we heard was elastic sonic material; that is, it reached into our ears and our bodies, making us part of the orchestra of vibrations in the sound field. "We are re-transmitters!" I said. "We are re-radiators and re-absorbers and reflectors of acoustical energy!"

"Pea?" asked the one, but instantly forgot the question.

Starlings turned a page of the sky.

The one asked the other whether she could stand all the faking at the brunch with War when everything they had said and done was only pretend-right. "You could tell," she said, a wintering sparrow, not very much like a child of eight.

I did not hesitate to be intrusive. I asked for them to itemize, and they did. I asked about the phatic communications of the waitstaff.

The one said that sometimes there was a sucking-through-teeth sound that came from a white-breasted male waitstaff, and, with my assistance, she demonstrated its volume and endurance.

The one said that sometimes there was a cough-chuckle from waitstaff at the time of order-taking, and I was able to identify this as being not unlike the cuck-cuck calls of chipmunks.

The Biltmore Inn hostperson's high voice produced a chirping sound specific to a creature with fifty-five teeth in its left wing; such a creature frequently spreads its wing covers, shuts them, and as they slowly close, its scraper calls out "tickatickaticktick-atickatickaticka" — many tickatickas of stridulation. I was disappointed to learn that my pupils had not been aware of more of the hostperson sounds, but then that is often the case since many notes are ultrasonic, too high to be audible to two small things.

The other said that the really old waitstaff looked like old opossums. ("You can tell if they're old by their frost-bit ears," I explained.) The other also reported that these opossums had a call: "Andyouhoney? Andyouhoney?"

The older said firmly to the younger, "It's not what Pea was asking about."

That was true: I was asking about the sounds that did not take the shape of words.

"And were there stridulations of any kind from waitstaff?" I asked. I was impatient for them to master identification of such sonic markers.

The one said that sometimes stridulations came from young and old waitstaff. Together, we discerned that these stridulations were the rubbing-together of crisp pants or pantyhose that occurred during delivery of food. After compensating for frequency, one would assign the sounds a relative loudness of 4, approximately 0.25 sones.

"And of what temperature were the sounds?" I asked as we came within a hundred feet of our campsite.

The other froze in place. "Pea," she said. She had been the first to hear. "Pea!" she shouted.

A bear grunted, "Gaaaaooohhh!" within twenty yards of us. We could not see her in the late afternoon light. We could hear her huff, stamp, make the bowel-guttering sounds a large female will make to keep the attention of her young.

We could not smell the bear. She was near — she warned, "Gggggaahoah-hoah-ggkkkaa!" — but she was downwind of us.

"She can smell us!" I shouted.

They knew what to do. Though they were frightened, they knew they must slowly back away from the origin of the sounds. They must produce noises, but not the mewling noises that might make a mother bear murderous. They must become big and unappetizing, human but on a superhuman scale. The first part involved holding hands, and raising their four arms overhead, and standing on their toes. The challenge of being unappetizing involved disco dance movements in which they imitated my raised right knee, my raised left knee, my forward-and-back shoulder-swagger.

Then came the quiet.

I did my railroad-crossing move with my arms. They moved with me. Needless to say, we had practiced all of these evasive maneuvers.

There was a snort far inside the quiet.

The other trembled, and the one.

"Pea?" asked the other.

"Pea?" asked the one.

A light step sound. Another. Another light step. She was still not visible, but she was coming, and at about the time of late afternoon she said she would. She was laughing, though she was ashamed of her laughing and was trying to stop.

She was in our path.

"This bear," I said, "is my older sister Elaine."

Elaine held out her arms as if the one or the other would be foolish enough to hug her. She held them out longer, and I stepped into them and closed my arms around her in order to lightly crunch her ribs and say, "I didn't believe you would really show up only so I could tell you in person to leave me alone." She made an eeking, pained sound I appreciated because as a child (over sixty years earlier) she had often caused me to eek in the same way.

"You should be more careful of bears," said Elaine to the children as she shrugged me off.

I said, "You found our campsite."

"Found it. The walk nearly killed me — old knees — old feet — old—"

"My sister," I said, "believes she has come to visit us. She believes we will welcome her visit."

"Yes," said Elaine with a mechanical formality meant to mock Samantha Peabody, "I — am — your — visi — tor." She did not yet again hold her arms out pointlessly, but she bent down to the children, and she asked, "Will you tell me your names?"

The older said, "Betty," and the younger said, "Janet." They did not sound kindly. The tone of the one was the turning-aside tone, and the tone of the other was the scornful echo. Inside me I made a field recording. Inside me were so many field recordings made through the seasons I "lost" children in these mountains. I did not and do not now lie to myself that I objectively evaluated what I collected; what I collected is poetry that degenerated to science under my successful scrutiny and reverted to song under my failing love.

"They are here to hear," I said to Elaine.

"Elaine," I said, "has closed earlids. She can hear but she is not a listener."

When they looked at her, I could see through their eyes how

my salt-and-pepper hair was like my sister's: rasped and short, sealed close to our heads, oily as if coated against moisture and cold.

The alert silence of the two and my own precisionist silence caused Elaine to ask, "What?"

I staked her to the ground with my stare. She wouldn't hear the sound, of course, but we did: reverberating through the chirping of the field crickets, and through the seed-falling and seed-sailing sounds and the sounds of wheezing does and grunting bucks, through the almost noiseless breeze-shiftings of frass and fecula under leaves and twigs: the commentary.

"Three," said the one.

"Two," said the other, and she was right, she knew it.

During that time of year on Desnos Creek whippoorwills sang, *These old hills — these old hills — these old —* these old. And from a different perch of longing, other whippoorwills sang, *Sold hills — sold hills — sold — sold — sold.*

Elaine said, "Samantha, I'm —"

She had spooked the whippoorwills, had ruined the transmission.

The children and I gave her frowns. To ruin the transmission was a serious infraction of our code.

" — pretty hungry, to be honest."

As if she had caused it with her noise, the clouds burst. There are moments in these woods when one element that totally withheld its response to another suddenly releases it like a train screaming out of a tunnel.

"Whoa!" said Elaine.

Freezing rain whirled through the shrubs and trees: coming through instead of coming down.

The older huddled so tightly over the younger that they were one creature bent at the waist and low to the ground when they came to the tent entrance.

The rain stung like buck-shot yellow jackets. As soon as they had frisked each other in order to avoid introducing foreign matter into our tent, the children went in. Outside, Elaine reacted poorly to me frisking her and to my insistence that she frisk me.

In the most intimidating voice I could muster, I said, "You're leaving in the morning, do you understand?"

The rain ended after less than eighty seconds. I was still standing very close to Elaine. She said, "You have to be such a bitch?" and slap-frisked my hips, and lifted her palms and forearms toward me, and said, "Huh?"

I picked the golden stars from her palms and her damp sweater sleeves. "Witch hazel blossoms," I said. "And watch your mouth with these two. I mean it."

"Do you watch *your* mouth with them?" she asked.

"No," I said.

Inside the tent, she asked, "They bloom? This time of year?"

"And they uncork like popguns," I said.

"Tell her about witch hazel," I asked the two.

Instead of talking about that, we opened the large thermos of hot water, taking sips, offering it last to Elaine. She wanted to know why we did not make tea, and she told us about the various kinds of tea she liked most — she wanted to know why we did not have pretzels or crackers, and she told us about how the simple generic *Laura Lynn* brand saltines were her favorite — she said it was a small tent, wasn't it — she said it sure got dark fast this time of year — she asked if the dark bothered them, and answered for them that they needed better light inside the tent, better light would make it less scary, so she said — she said that a bigger tent would be a good thing, wouldn't it — she supposed it would not be as cozy, though — she went on, a more and more curious expression on her face, the evidence of an unanswerable question burying itself. She said, "I'm hungry."

"We ate," said the other.

"We only eat in the middle of the day," said the one.

"And dinner?" my sister asked, "What about dinner?"

Elaine's nature led her to hear neither the voices in the world around her nor those farther away. Like many who are not listeners, she could never hear her own voice, her own words, though she had perfect hearing, though she was fluent in her speech. In that oblivious state, Elaine continually made up a version of her own and others' past and present discourse.

She did not feel she must make more effort to hear. She was unaware that many of her own extraordinary sensitivities to others instinctively developed from compensation for her unlistening nature.

Her many friends, the telling not the tweeting generation, received loving connection from her that was inspiring to witness. In a time of momentary or, for that matter, monumental difficulty, she was the one old person you would want at your side, unless you needed dialogue, unless you wished for the giving sounds and the offering sounds, for the listening.

Why was it so impossible for me to forgive her for that? I am human. I am awfully human. I would never insult animal and vegetal life by calling my own unfair judgments and bad behavior "inhuman." In one hundred thousand years of existence as their mother earth's brutal demi-human horde, humans have committed matricide, have transformed her clay to shit.

"You need food," said the one to Elaine, who did not hear her.

I knew Elaine did not have rain gear, and I offered her mine, the pants and hooded jacket, so the two of us could walk downcreek to the food.

The children insisted on coming along.

When we left the tent, I said firmly, "Complete quiet, Elaine."

Rime ice glistened all around us. It slipped from the warming chitinous branch sleeves with the clicking sound of false teeth. We could hear a few crows, a few woodpeckers. Their sounds deepened and their bodies darkened the forest. These friends without primary consciousness made no effort — for our sake — to be conscious. At night when my love for them was purest, I could more easily believe that they had none of the burdens of a sense of self.

A raccoon chortled at us from outside our bright cones of rain-struck light, and Elaine said, "Jesus!" and told me that I should give her a flashlight — that she might trip — that we should have an extra, and said she wondered if Betty and Janet had ever heard of the Boy Scout motto, "Be prepared," which reminded her that she could never remember the Girl Scout motto, but she felt it must be "Keep Your Boy Scout Prepared" — and she said she was just joking — but that Samantha knew the motto, those were the kinds of things Samantha knew — that you never got anything out of Samantha unless you asked, and — and —

As soon as there was at last a slight pause, I asked the two if they would retrieve Elaine some crackers and turkey jerky from our food cache. They gladly left.

We followed from a distance, catching up at a place where whip-poorwills could be heard.

The two gave her small portions. The two did not like her. I reinforced their negative attitude by asking Elaine in their hearing whether her new husband had fallen silent yet. I did not say aloud that the natural outcome of her stubborn virtual deafness was that the people around her experienced tampening and, next, diminishing attentiveness, then successive forms of canceling out, and silent, distant communion. This did not take long. She had silenced her first husband within the first year of their thirty-year marriage. He moved inward. And deeper inward. Like all of us who loved Elaine, he found he truly loved her in that deepest place to which his silence led him. And I believe he found he loved the person he himself was in that silent instar stage of development; in any case, that was my own experience of knowing Elaine. And it was my experience — I thought it must have been his, too — that as time passed he loved her more intensely but loved her more profoundly from afar, which caused him to eventually love himself more — but from afar. How is it possible that I recapitulated Elaine's path in my own marriage to Robert, making him feel ever more alone from our first to our last day together? I saw into myself through Elaine, which meant that I did not want to see her at all.

Elaine was a success story. The textbook materials she could memorize — all the materials she refused to actually hear a teacher present or interpret — were inexhaustible. Ours was the era of teaching as an art and a science; the '40s and '50s were not yet the corporate era of teaching to the test. Mature teachers treated her badly since such a female talking-machine seemed especially horrifying to them, but outside of school, everyone else praised her, promoted her. Yes, I was jealous of my brilliant sister to whom the golden slipper was perennially affixed by genius peers, by princes, by the fellowship committees, the loan officers, the executive boards.

The two led us back to camp. Occasionally, one or the other would glance back at Elaine and give her the ass-wipe look, since Elaine's nonstop vocalizations meant we would hear nothing in the woods during this walk or, most likely, until she left.

We reorganized our tent space so that Elaine could be in the center. She could not understand how she would fit. We explained to her that she would have to curl on her side and compress herself. She could not understand why Samantha Peabody decided the sleep time — could not understand how she would get up in the night if she needed — she could not comprehend why people believed camping was at all enjoyable. Because she had not heard one word of her own words, she asked again, "How will I get up in the night and go out of the tent and water the garden and come back in?"

"Slowly. And silently," said the older one. The younger echoed her: "Slowly. And silently."

They asked me to play my harmonica.

I asked Elaine if she could be quiet for one full measure of music.

She asked if I would freak out if she did not.

The one said, "Samantha Peabody will definitely freak out."

"She will," said the other.

The one said, "We could hear a ghost story."

"You brought books?" asked Elaine.

They explained that Samantha Peabody did not allow books on the sonic adventure.

An exchange of glances occurred between the one and the other. Of course, as in early October, the two things had brought books about which they believed Samantha Peabody was unaware. She had thwarted their efforts to read, which does not mean she prevented them from reading at times they were not in her company. She allowed them to preserve their sense that they held a secret.

Elaine said, "Children who love books —"

"It's all right," said the one, wishing not to be exposed.

Elaine asked me, "But you have your books here?"

"I bring an entire box of them with me for all my adventures," I said. "I couldn't live a day without them." And in response to her glaring, I answered, "I am a self-disciplined adult. A trained bioacoustician. The children, who naturally see-hear, must go without books in their thirteen weeks with me or they will not hear-see, and they will most certainly not hear."

"That is just weird," she said. "You are weirder than ever. You talk weird, even."

The two affixed themselves to me the way they did at the first part of the night. When it was time to wear them like two parts of a casing, I wore the two things.

"No ghost story tonight," I said. "Elaine frightens easily."

"True," said Elaine. "Samantha and I heard the Hansel & Gretel story when we were little, really little, and I — it was a horrible story, and it gave me nightmares."

"I love my sister," I said.

"And it still does," she said.

"You do?" asked the one.

"You do," said the other.

I had made stories a regular element of the sonic adventure. Each story I told the children, I offered in its natural form. A good haunted forest story takes practice, because one must perfect the roaring-fire parts and the full-moon whispering parts of adults betraying children, the moans, screams, creaks, the scraping parts, the sighing parts of water intent on drowning children trying to cross. The thumps. The fear-triggering, vertigo-inducing thumps. The shovelings and buryings and the gruntings in the voices of adults practiced in discarding or consuming their young. The actual narrative has the smallest value, but when one is trying to offer hainting, one will lean on affective creation of timbre, of lifts and breaks in voice, not providing credible narrative construction but the uncanny fantastic.

"I love my sister," said Elaine. Apparently she felt they must respond to this odd truth.

"We're old ladies, you know."

"And?" I asked.

"And. Well, ask your mother. To love for a long time is —"

"Impossible," I said.

She said, "*Almost,*" and she rubbed her knees with her hands, which trembled slightly.

"It will be a long night." I recommended that they use the earplugs I had issued them in October. These ear condoms were ribbed, able to block sound according to their depth of insertion.

"No music?" asked the other. She had a grip on my right knee, and I do not know why I did not request that she let go.

Samantha Peabody, I explained, did not offer music that is interruptible. I knew this insult to my sister would not register with Elaine, and I am confident the two things recognized that I was merely reasserting my rules.

Elaine said, "They like me — you should let them like me — and then they would like me more. People always said I was good with them, with children — with the ones that are out of diapers, with the —"

Her voice reminded me of circumstances in which it is necessary to use the 0.02 depth setting on the earplugs. The Phon-Aid device, which helps one regain the lost sense of measuring sound intensity, is useful in training the ear of the sonic adventurer.

With the convenient use of their P-A devices, the two continued to look at Elaine's constantly moving mouth. They eventually looked away, looked at each other, entered silence's mutualities as good monks and certain lucky sonic initiates might.

For half an hour, Elaine plunged into the issues between her and me: I wished to separate myself from her; impossibly, I wished for her to know that I loved her and would always love her, but I wanted to be apart from her. I wished for her to forgive me for this choice. I wished for her to forgive me if I failed at this and at a later time wanted entry again into her life.

I was grateful, I told her, that she came to me here in the mountains, here at the threshold of my own choices, and did not make me come to her in the city.

In September, I had written to her about my plan to begin separating from all human contact. I knew that she would only half-read the letter because the half-hearer is always an erasing reader taking in the vague contexts but never the subtexts and the codes of language.

She said, "You are unnaturally depressed. The longer you go with no one telling you that you are depressed, the more you are depressive, Sam."

"I cannot disagree," I said, six syllables wasted on her.

"We're old women now, Sam. The time's passing faster. What if I die? What if you — out in the middle of nowhere —"

She rambled on in cleft sentences.

"What you need is to let me start over, and you need to start over yourself, people do that, you can do that, what you did was you just went away, you were a goer-away from the time you were a kid, and when I — What I did was I did the best I could at everything — What is the crime in that? — and you went away pretty far like our parents went away from each other and couldn't come back but stayed in to the bitter end — and what I do is to make good — and when your —"

Her voice softly catching, she said, "When your Robert died, what you did was to go away from everybody and everything. You're still going — going away. What I did was try to say things that might help. I'm trying — I try."

"You are correct," I said. "You said words. You say words."

"God help me. My heart is —"

I did not say, *You could have just shut up so I could find you.* I did not say, *If I could have found you through your blizzard of words, you could have been some refuge to me. And when you divorced, I could have been some refuge to you.*

"You've never said what exactly went wrong between me and you, Samantha. I don't know what went wrong. When Mom and Dad used to ask — and when other people, too, used to

ask — I didn't know what to say. You were — I don't know —
unnatural. When we were teenagers people wanted to know
whether there was something wrong with my little sister, my
sour, unlovable sister. My friends Robert and Carla — well,
we were five years older than you — and Amelia four years —
and we were like our own closed friend club — and that wasn't
right, I know that — and you were just never going to agree to
be a member and so, Sam — so — why — do you know what I
mean? — why give you a key?"

Not a chance. There was not a chance to say and to be heard.

The two had fallen asleep, and through the night I listened to
Elaine, tried to console her, listened, listened, listened, tried to
hear her and what her swarm of words sought. I tried not to
allow my brain to simply select the wished-for words. I thought
of the kinds of keys I held and the ones held by Elaine, of the
doors I had closed, the ones she had closed. It was no different
between her and me than between me and Robert's sister Amelia, our affinities in magnetic flux.

Two hours before sunrise, she finally took up less space on the
center of the tent floor. She slept contracted into a tight ball. I
watched her sleep. Then I helped her get up. Slowly. Silently.
The children had not woken up yet. They had missed the chance
to explain to Elaine about the golden stars of the witch hazel
in which there are large black seeds that feel like bits of bone.
When the stars explode — with a croupy spitting sound — the
seeds can bullet trees thirty feet away.

I held Elaine's hand as we walked down the trail away from
the campsite. She did not like walking in the dark. I knew the
footing in this darkness, but she did not take my hand when

I offered.

At the trailhead parking lot, she mumbled aloud to herself. About what was worse: Was it worse to . . . Was it worse to . . . the worst thing was . . . the worst thing was . . .

I listened. As she got into her car she was still talking to herself.

Twelve years have passed and I have not seen Elaine. In March and September I receive her letters through Drummer. I understand that for Elaine to write to me is difficult because of arthritis in her arms and hands. Her letters are inchoate and all-but-illegible. Like a fool, I respond to them.

December 4 — 10, 2003

We had spent the sunrise hours north of our campsite at a familiar abandoned beaver pond a considerable distance off-trail. Clouds with hoarfrost edges made the sunlight advance and delay in its quivering path through the water. The one and the other were walking with me around the pond in an outward-moving pattern approximating the rippling lines of a topographic map. With each of our eight circumambulations, we were wordlessly asking December in the Pisgah to allow us to hear.

More than once, I had glared at them both for not touching their feet down more quietly so that we could hear the wee-zee of the black and white warblers, the risible song of red-eyed vireos: where-are-you-here-here-I-AM. We stopped so that I could show them again the stride, the slight bending of the knees, the vulpine carriage of limbs and body and neck and head. When we resumed walking, I glared at them for listening to their own kit fox movements.

According to my instruction, Carla had purchased identical pewter-gray down vests for them, and black, flannel-lined cotton pants, and light, felt-sole black shoes. I was dressed in identical apparel, including ear-flap woolen caps acquired for us by Drummer. The caps were perfect for warming the delicate instrument of the auricle before exposing it.

*

The night before this hike, we had been woken up by the sound of screaming predation. And by the other animal sounds that follow: the cries of the creature hunted, trapped, dragged along the ground, sometimes carried in mid-air, wounded only enough to be brought alive to the feast; the creature's raptured grunting as it is torn apart.

The two had said, "Pea. Pea?" They had whimpered and shivered and shed hot tears.

We had heard these banquet sounds more than once in October and November, but we had not spoken about them.

At the very moment I invited them to enter my sleeping bag, they shimmied down to clamp onto my legs. They were enough like my own flesh that their almost-nakedness and mine were no more unusual than crystalline spicules forming upon a cold twig.

I had held them, nudged at them in order to comfortably position their bodies and mine in our casing. My body stored up the nourishment of that feeling. I recover some — a little of the feeling — as I write all of this down for me, for them, for the earth as the author of them and me.

When the other said, "You're *rough!*" I said, "You bark! And it is my job to get your back-fur in my teeth and move you where you belong."

"But — actually —" said the one. The fear had slightly retreated from her, and her tone was playful.

I liked this: not being able to see their faces and not having my face seen. There was no specific visual data that I had to select out in order to hear them and to hear myself, and therefore no significant temporal misinformation. "You," I said to the one, "are relatively happy. A moment ago a hawk was ripping apart a young woodpecker out cheerfully waltzing on the snow. That was only a few minutes ago — I estimate five to six minutes ago — and you sounded like a sucking drainpipe. And now there is a jocund tone coming from you —" I wanted the right word — "pinging from you."

"Yeah," said the younger to the older, "you're *pinging*."

I pointed out that they were both pinging, that there was a tighter tension in the sound of them and also a slacker tension, like a note in tune and a note de-tuned a half step. I asked if they heard it in my voice: I, too, was afraid when I heard those ripsaw flesh-consuming sounds; I was thrilled by them.

After a long silence, the other said, "Betty's got glasses."

The one said, "I got them before Thanksgiving. She's jealous."

The other said, "War paid for them. He was sorry for us about everything and he —"

"He said he has two different kinds of glasses, so he can see everything he needs to see."

I took this in. I decided against responding to this bit of Warren information.

I said, "The sounds frightened you. That's understandable, acceptable. You are both in a pattern of avoidance."

"Am not," said the other.

I said, "We do not easily accept that we are human and animal enough to respond positively to the sounds of devouring."

"Then why do you act like you can't see?" said the other to her sister. "All of a sudden you act like you can't see good."

I said, "We don't find it easy to accept that we are animal and human enough to feel excitement in being the devourers."

The one, as if on an isolated, exalted perch, said, "They're perfect for my face."

"They are," I said. I had noticed them earlier in the day. They had metal frames, were light-adaptive. They had a realistic copper sunflower on each stem. The wealthy boyfriend-judge could purchase such expensive, stylish glasses for Carla's oldest daughter.

"You noticed?" asked the one.

"They are," said the other sadly, "they're perfect." The energy had drained from her. Her hand moved across my knees to seek her sister's hand. "Betty is pretty — like nobody else," she said.

How do sisters forget all the mothering they give each other? All the tenderness they practice and perfect, the meat they timidly and then terrifyingly rip from each other's bones?

The younger child fell asleep. The older verged into sleep and fought it, verged again. She said, "Pea?"

"I'm here."

"I just turned eight."

"Well, then," I said, "you were not eight from birth."

She giggled. "I turned eight on November nineteenth."

"I do not hold your age against you. Your brain is still developing and particularly your phonoreceptors, and I feel fortunate that I am your sonic mentor at this time in which the left hemisphere of your very rubbery brain and the complex mechanisms of your sense organs are trainable."

I wanted to hear her. I also wanted to hear the fluttering of the pine siskins in the thickets and the meadow mice scrambling on their familiar paths. Shrews were out night hunting, and I wanted to hear them.

"You thought I was already eight."

"That is true."

"My mother told you that."

"Your graymother is a liar — I mean, a lawyer — after all."

"She doesn't talk to me like you do, " she said.

"I have no doubt that is true."

"She doesn't like how you talk bad."

"I curse entirely too much."

"She doesn't like it. Like *really*."

We both stopped to hear: the wind fracturing the smallest joints of twigs, the bead-clacking of winter berries on certain shrubs and trees. In this small December bower in the Pisgah, thick scales guard the tender buds. The wind makes a furring sound when it ruffles the wooly, resinous scales.

"My brain," I said, "talks directly to your brain. I do not have a repulsive Judge Warren here displaying himself to me as I try to communicate with you."

"That is true, no doubt." I felt inexpressibly pleased that she could imitate my voice with such microtonally perfect ventriloquation.

"We are hiking to the beaver pond tomorrow. We will sleep now," I said. Gusts of wind caused the starlight piercing the skeletal tree canopy to pulse in the fabric of our tent.

She was restless though exhausted. In that pupate light, she fought sleep. She said, "Janet's six. Mom didn't lie about her." One of her warm, small feet pushed my callused large foot. I took mental note of her coldness. I remembered her sister's cold hand, and made another mental notation: *socks, gloves.*

"Janet's birthday is October seventeenth," she whispered. "I — "

"Goodnight," I said. Firmly.

I had discouraged the two from saying that they loved me. Their love had traveled through them to me, and still does — in sound, in crumbs of sound.

❊

Reversing our movement, we walked around and toward the

shallow pond. The bed of it was a dense layering of leaves and twigs, of saturated berries and acorns and shagbark hickory nuts, of blighted buds and shrub scale and animal underfur. This affected the drum of the pond surface responding to the wind. Together we subtracted from the soundscape the wind luffing our clothing. We subtracted the sounds made by our mouths and nasal cavities. As much as possible, we each subtracted from our singular hearing our accurate and inaccurate perceptions of what the other two heard. We subtracted October and November sonic memories of this pond, and subtracted the educing fantasies that cause a sensitive hearer to hear what is there, inside, but not there, outside. This sound subtraction is one of many procedures I taught them for refreshing their hearing. I had trained them so effectively that they would have little need for the Phon-Aid devices, except at home.

The one asked about the little balls of jelly in the pond, and I explained transpiration, how the trees rained their oily and pitchy waters down. "If we chose to stand in this pond today all day and tonight all night," I said, "the trees would rain lightly and constantly on us, and we would hear their releasing sounds."

"And we would be gloppy," said the other.

We subtracted her voice. We subtracted my voice. When they took my hands up, they did not place theirs inside mine. They placed mine inside theirs.

*

(Surely you understand now — but how could you have known then? — that this hand-holding allowed me to walk more lightly under the oaks, to hear you and to better hear me inside me.)

*

Microbursts of wind slipped back the sheet of the pond and disturbed its sleeping body and rustled its bedding. In the thickets
near us, finches split and spat and spewed cedar berries. Though
inside and unseen, raccoons conversed at the exit to their home.
The wind caused the mouth of the exit to sough, and, welcoming this, we began to hear the in-whispering of tree boluses,
the inverted echoing cups of stones having the smallest hiding
spaces beneath them, the resonant silences in empty bird and
wasp nests. After hearing the rhythm of the earth's soft-palate
sounds, we could hear the timbre of its hard-palate sounds: the
empty shells and keels and the tight-fisted fleshless ribs of dead
creatures no bigger than seeds and pods. The bright green coat-
ing on the north side of the trees, the Mardi-Gras-green algae
scum, and the green felt vaucheria on the surface of the soil: the
sounds were these green colors.

Whenever he wanted to emerge from within me, he did so with
such force that I almost said aloud to the two things: My husband liked to hold my hand. He liked mine inside his. And for
all our twenty-nine years together, that had thrilled me.

At the first appointment in the massive office of the lawyer
whom I hired with the express instruction to eviscerate him,
he had reached across in order to ask of me: that I guide him,
his hand in mine, into the voracious mouth of his lifelong law-
yer-friend Carla. I did not. I did not take up his hand. I am the
human species. I am not the clay but the cracked bowl; I have
made myself of use, and my heart all but useless. At any time
that I have had the opportunity to show no mercy to some-

one whom I believed deserved no mercy, all my instincts for cruelty have murdered the last traces of my own true nature.

They pulled. They pulled again.

We were in such a delicately balanced tripod that they almost tumbled us down. The one rocked like a daruma doll. She shriek-laughed, and that caused me to say to them, "You have ruined the transmission." I privately felt that perhaps we had realized the transmission.

During our days of sonic adventure, the two sometimes recognized my secret-most thoughts. We did not, of course, hear alike, but I believe that our hearing was in such communion we could be carried beyond the limits of normal human auscultation. We could not hear each other's thoughts — I do not mean that. I mean we could hear the re-sounding of the thought sounding in each of us.

"Where are they?" asked the other.

I knew she meant the beavers that had labored like factory workers at this pond.

"They've gone."

Too amazed to ask it as a question, the one said, "Pea. They made all of it."

"The whole dam thing," I said.

The two were more or less obliged to laugh. They did.

I told them that this would have been a dreamed-of setting for beavers, that all of the pond's features were suited perfectly to them creating their own ecosystem there, thriving, reproducing, accruing resources and, eventually, excesses of resources.

"When you hear them at work," I said, "they sound like they're partying hard."

"It makes them happy," said the one.

"Awful happy. But there is a high burn-out rate for beavers. Once they strip everything around them, their impoundment fails them. And the entire tribe goes to the next dreamlike place. And they repeat their offenses."

Later, as we ate turkey jerky and saltines, the one asked me to tell about my husband. After all, I had brought him up, hadn't I? During our previous days together in October and November, I had offered strictly the outline of my life with him: yes, married at thirty-four, 1969; yes, love; no, no children; he had an older brother Tim (in Wheeling, West Virginia) and a younger sister Amelia (in Asheville); yes, a home, which was a small, old home of nine-hundred square feet, for "Sam & Rob," which is what everyone called us; he, the librarian in the same elementary school where my sister Elaine was a teacher; yes, it was a divorce that was very terrible. 1998: when they were five and three years old, respectively.

They had heard from their graymother Carla: divorce was very terrible. I assumed they did not know that she could make it terrible beyond imagining.

I did not tell them of Robert's death in 1999. A migraineur for fifty years, he had always said that the worst migraines made him certain he was having a brain stroke. He had always joked that on the day he actually had a fatal stroke, he would find himself saying, "*Not* a migraine!"

The school had been notified, and Elaine had gone to the hospital. She phoned me and said that after the initial stroke on that October morning, and before the killing massive strokes the next day, he had begged her to bring me there so that he could see me. It felt cruel — perfectly — to respond by saying that he should contact my lawyer.

I did not reveal to the two that their mother had been my divorce attorney, that she had adjudicated Robert's will, making sure to assign me all that remained, that she had ignored the request of his sister Amelia to have some sentimental belongings given to her: a childhood picture of him on a snowy soccer field with his father holding his hand, two special books from his library, a watch his parents gave him at high school graduation.

What a good lawyer Carla was: that she could make his sister pay for all the funeral arrangements with the little money he had left her in his will; that she could visit me on the burial day, give me the key to the "recovered items" in the storage garage. What a good lawyer: that she could report the satisfaction in sending a man naked to his grave, digging him up and skinning him, handing the skin to me, the woman he had betrayed with another lover.

The one asked, "When it's time for us to hear, what time is it for beavers?"

I said, "You asked about him, about Robert."

"But —" said the other who was actually saying, But we didn't ask for so much, okay?

I touched the lobes of their ears. I liked to touch their supple mechanisms for absorbing and attuning. "There is a domain of time humans inhabit. Sounds configure this domain. And this domain positions and contrapositions sound. We are surrounded and directed inside time's sphere and its flow."

"Okay," said the other, who could always make her way past mere knowing into the awe of whelming-feeling.

"If beavers made clocks," I said, "they would be nothing like the clocks humans make."

I rearranged their hair. I did not like the old-fashioned bob of their honey-brown hair, an adult bob.

"And?"

"And?"

They withdrew themselves from my touch.

As we cabled our food up, loose items jingled inside the food storage canister, and the compartments of the earth's body and our own bodies lifted and lowered us. Sound, after all, penetrates the structures from which it is generated. It moves audibly through the earth's crust and atmosphere. Absorbed by densities and amplified by concavities, sound percusses the general skin surfaces of the outer ear, the pinna and concha, the specific soundfields of the helix and antihelix, tragus and antitragus; the auricle does not reconcile signals on their way to the eardrum, but infinitely recomposes them. Sound, a natural syntax, asks to be re-heard whenever it is "read." This, my little album-confession-storybook, asks, *Have you heard?*

We looked through the crown dieback made by atmospheric deposition. Hundreds of churning glacial eyes. Blue. Clear.

January 2 — 8, 2004

I told them that I wanted to hear the red squirrels grunting and barking. The red squirrels complain and complain — and sing — and complain some more that conditions might not be safe at the moment for singing. But then. But then. But then.

I wanted to hear the newest hits of the black-capped chickadees, one of my favorite bands. This time of year they changed their sound from "dee-dee—dee-dee—dee-dee" to "fee-bee-fee-bee-fee-bee." The nuthatches sometimes took the stage with them, and it got — well — there's no other word for it: wild.

"You think that is humorous?" I asked the younger child. "I want to hear all of it. I mean it." Sitting inside our tent, we were passing the cup, sipping the hot water I had boiled on the camp-stove outside where I had listened to the creek's bank-licking and to the card-shuffling sound of the wind in the beeches and the white oaks that still have their leaves in winter. I had listened to the *gggha* and *bha* and bha-gggha-uhrrr vocalizations of bear cubs inside a hollow tree across the creek. "I'm unsure. You cannot be sure," I said to the two, "but I believe the cubs are still learning the language," and I explained that one needed to assume that the young — fledgling birds and newborn mice and young raccoons — were not born with the ability to instantly articulate their song and call. "They learn. They listen and they learn." It was just as probable that there were skunks under that hollow tree or bobcats inside, but they sounded like inarticulate bear cubs. If they were young skunks they were amateur vocalizers. I wanted to hear this. I wanted the two to hear this.

"I like the sounds," said the older.

"They're chill," said the younger.

I am old enough now that I can appreciate what they have added to my own vocabulary. A sound can be chill. A person can be chill.

At some point during the Christmas holidays, the other and the one had learned the many nuances of identifying "chill" and enacting "chill." They told me that they learned from a television program how to dance "like Kylie and Missy." The two were certain I would not know who the famous Kylie and Missy were; it was satisfying to them when I fell silent.

They showed me the essential movements. The arm and leg movements imitated certain predaceous aquatic insects with raptorial front legs. I did not respond though I was fascinated.

I did not say the dancing was chill. I am saying that now.

I like the term, and the accompanying expression, "chill wid it." That a sonic or visual or tactile or gustatory or olfactory experience, that an action or concept, that the phenomenal and the epiphenomenal could be felt as a temperature: marvelous.

I use the term in my conversations with myself. Before I began to write this morning, to place these memory specimens in these pages, I looked at my field notes from that year, swiftly compared them with my field notes for this year. The word came to mind.

Chill.

The word summons the two who travel to me through twelve years of absence.

In my field observations I had noted the sniffing-purring and grinding-crunching noises of rabbits during the rabbit habit of chewing sumac twigs and bark. I had twice noted the trees sounding animal-like — sipping and chirruping and sucking and croaking and chip-too-chipping when the bow of the wind bounced upon or drew against the diamond-shaped bark of white ash or the long-ridged bark of chestnut. I had twice noted a bird I could not name who imitated the catbirds who disappeared each year in October and who had a whispering song something like *tsoon-tsoon — tsoon-tsoon*. I had twice noted the one-dimensional vocalizations of juncos whose countershaded bodies make them seem neither round nor solid, a kind of snow and snow shadow in the winter woods.

"Do not let them LOOK!" I had written as a teaching goal. Vegetal can sound animal, animal can sound vegetal; what looks flat can sound flat, what looks round sounds round but falsely. There is now no need to write down my teaching goals, but I do. I would like to stop going on and on. I would like to quit this incessant impulse to teach. These woods, my steady companion, ask me to hear. What I have to say matters not at all, and I suppose that compels me to always spill instead of pour this whole account of that year. Like no other in my life.

It is January 2017 and I am here in my tent, which is my writing room, records room, library and reading room, planetarium and enclosed sun porch, music studio, bedroom, sitting room, walk-in closet; my supply and storage locker, my domed space of eight feet in circumference, my threshold, my laboratory, my abyss. And I am reading and refining my 2003–2004 notes, and many times as I read, I say to myself, "Chill," and answer myself, "Chill."

I have noted that in less than a century, less than a billionth of a second in geologic time, global warming has confused the bears here in the Pisgah. They do not quite know the season around them, which is to say that they do not quite know they are bears. I have noted that humans, likewise, are confused about whether they have a human brain or a beaver brain; this profound confusion has occurred in approximately the infinitesimal span of .000001 of the one-hour equivalent that humans have occupied this planet since the universe's beginningless Big Kiss.

I am disturbed about the bears: they are erratic now in their seasons of birthing cubs, of hibernating, of mating.

"I, too, appreciate the sounds," I said. "And the mating sounds. And the courting sounds. If animals mate at the wrong time, as they do more and more often in our era of ecological collapse, there are fucking sounds."

✳

(Do you two read this now and feel repulsed that I inexcusably taught such very young children to make use of the term "fucking" and its appositive words and phrases?)

✳

We agreed that for our January week of sonic adventure we should concentrate upon the courtship and mateship and fuckship sounds of the season. Our agreement was contingent upon them lying to their mother about our course of study. This plan gave them such notable pleasure that they readily elaborated upon my recommended misinformation. I suggested that they should report freshly to her upon an older lesson I had offered about sonic ecological succession, a topic of instruction in November.

The one said, "We'll tell her about climax forests," and the other said, "And how about the crying lichen?"

"What?" I asked. Already, I liked what I heard. Liars with uninformed but forming self-awareness are my favorite fictionalists.

"About how they cry when they can't grow," said the other.

I had taught them about certain lichen that might be considered "signal lichen" since they cannot — or will not — grow where there is pollution. Needless to say, the lichen make no audible sound. "Right," I said, "tell her about the pitiful sounds of the Crying Lichen."

"Have you heard?" said the one.

"It is really sad," said the other. "They never stop crying."

I gulped the last of our warm water. We dressed, organized our living space, left the tent.

Outside, hanging from the lowest limbs of black locust trees and rhododendron were two small pairs of pale green wool mittens and pale green wool socks, and one larger pair. This meant that Drummer had visited in the early morning, had crept in with the fog, and left the socks and mittens, then retreated, singing, "Sam Peabody! Sam Peabody!" so softly I could hear her in my dreams. I had asked her to acquire the articles of clothing so that I could give them to the two as special gifts. They would not have been easy to find. I suspected she had bought them in a cream or white color, and had dyed them so that they were exactly to my specifications. It was like her to find some for me, as well. It would be like her to have purchased an identical set for herself.

The two were grateful. They asked when, and so I shared that I had thought of this in November. They asked why, and so I shared my observation that they had many serious items of plumage but few silly items. They asked how, and so I shared that I had a friend, a two-day-a-year friend, very old, that I visited each March and September. Her cabin was often hidden under evening or morning mist, she was a drummer and the descendant of drummers, and, though I called her "Drummer," everyone in the hills where that mist is ever-present called her by other names, the names hill people give a mist-haint.

The tales were all similar.

One early morning when the cool fog settled upon the holler and its folds, when murmurs came from the hidden bowing heads of the trees, when the mummified words in our own thoughts mumbled from inside the mazes under hidden and half-hidden roots, an ancient fog arrived inside the fog.

The creature we called Silvershawl appeared.

Some called her Old Broom for she swept you from your hiding places. Some called her Mistress Ash for she was fire's ghost. And always she whispered the same question . . .

Hers was a dreaded and welcomed singing, one pure voice, an evil chorus, and inside us it danced and disappeared, it pushed us apart and gathered us in.

And always Silvershawl asked the same question.

Well. You know.

✢

During our January week, when we saw fog, the one would say, *"And always Silvershawl asked the same question,"* and the other would say, *"Well. You know,"* and we did not need to say, *Have you heard?* So, we did not.

✢

When we heard the sounds of horny woodchucks out in search of rutting females talking estrousy trash to each other, the younger would grin at the older with fulsome pleasure. But the pleasure was distinctly free of confinement to mere sexual reference. I have no doubt about this: it was sound their minds reached toward but did not grasp and reduce in ways they might have done if they were twelve and ten years old.

One afternoon we suspended both our mealtime and nap-time because we had the opportunity to observe a male gray squirrel repeatedly chasing a female, the two sounding like they were in bloodthirsty, exuberant battle, and the female tickering constantly though in modulating volume that made the male huff-cough-swallow-kuck, release and instantaneously regrip the tree trunk before vaulting to a limb above her.

We observed this patiently. The female would practically levitate her hindquarters in view of the male. I stated the obvious: "He likes that: her lordosis reflex." I allowed them to use their binoculars because they would definitely encounter this squirrel behavior again and they would have opportunity to listen without visual distraction.

After the seduction, we ate a light meal. Though they objected, I insisted they take a nap. One need not cancel naptime for the sake of science; for proof, consult the biographies of the famous nappers Muriel Wheldale Onslow, Rachel Louise Carson, and Florence Bascom.

I taught them Little Walter's "Temperature." I played harp, and we sang, "My baby give me a *high* temperature! My baby give me a high temperature!"

Huge had taught me to first find the ground of the song, the light rocking that sets a cadence before it introduces a drama inside the hearer's consciousness. He said to make the bass line my teacher for this, and if there was no bass line then to draw (and only sometimes blow) the notes according to the drum's cooking, and, if no drum, then to simmer down the flavor of the guitar's cleanest repeated riff. Don't imitate. Feel what it was before it was, and feel what it might become. He made me chase after the vocal phrase before gliding under it. The sound at first was mostly meant to be single-note, and meant to mostly come from the middle of the mouth or from the back of the mouth.

Huge and I had both gotten new teeth that last year before he died. My two front caps were thirty years past their expiration date, and they didn't fit my gums. He also had front teeth that needed to be replaced. We were illogically pleased about this serendipity. We smiled big at each other, satisfied that our embouchures were unaffected by the new dental hardware.

Flutter the valve of the throat real light. Tongue the note. Tap it. Try what it feels like to come in at the turn-around.

"I sang ninety-nine ..." and they repeated the phrase, and we set down the feel of it, the flow. And I stopped us.

I asked, "Have you heard?"

The other said, "Huh?"

"It sounds like the female gray squirrel." I made a squirrely figure with my harp, bending the third and vamping the fifth.

"That is the female quite exactly," said the one, lying precisely as if she were Samantha Peabody lying, and inflecting the words in such a way that she sounded like Samantha Peabody lying to Samantha Peabody.

"Exactly!" said the other.

We could definitely remember what we'd seen: the female and the male had stopped their mad chasing. The male took an alert stance on a high, long branch. He had nodded to another branch and kik-kucked and nodded again to the female close next to him.

Without really leaping, she had simply dropped herself to the next lowest branch, bounce-landed, did three or four barrel-turns.

She lightly bounded on the big branch below the male. She made a sound that could not accurately be called a mating sound. A claw-hammered banjo could make the sound she made if the banjo was furry and in perfect tune sexually. Tail-over-body-and-head, she lay prone on the branch and made the sound again — nothing like the sound my harp could ever make even if I were playing through an Astatic JT-30 microphone.

The two were sleepy. I wanted them to have their nap. I sang, "One-hundred-and-one when we kiss and dance — one-hundred-two for night romance," and they sang it after me. "One-hundred-three, four and five — it gets too warm to stay alive!"

I said, "You are both lying about my playing. I didn't even come close to the sound of the gray squirrel's mating sound. I was off. I was way off. I wanted to hear you tell me I played it right. You lied to me, and I am complicit in your lie."

The other's in-breath and her out-breath: I heard how something had flown there that would have landed.

"We are lying," I said. "We are liars."

The one gave me an impermissible (but well-deserved) get-over-it grunt.

Inside the tune, I played what I would call a gas burner, a few notes that sounded like the ring of flames igniting on an old gas stove. They were pure notes, the right whooshing notes. "You may close your eyes now," I said. "Close them over the sight of your own lying faces and over the sight of my face. Close them over the sight of other lying faces you have seen."

The tent was cold enough that we could see our breaths. I put on my new gloves and new socks, and I gave my unspoken approval for them to put on theirs. They were otherworld green in the ruffling afternoon light coming through the tent skin.

"One cannot close one's earlids, dear things. Remember that. Those of us who hear each other lie do not easily forget."

We had watched the male squirrel gaze down at the female. At the very instant they were on the verge of connection, she jumped up. She ran to the slenderest end of the branch and leaped onto another tree.

He had madly followed.

I regret writing that: "He had madly followed." I regret all of the above. To anthropomorphize is an aberrant compliment to human nature and an insult to animal nature. I feel more and more that this album I am making as a specimen album is not, in fact, an album at all, but a musician's fake book, a trick mirror, a chalkboard, an empty oven; or it is a long, overlong letter to myself and these woods inside and around me; or it is a teacher's monthly suicide note; or it is something I should give to no one though I will give it to the one and the other. I will.

The tent was less cold than when we entered. The two held me close. "There's no need to judge," I said, though they had closed their eyes and kept them closed. "Humans lie," I said. I thought of my own feeling that for some humans lying is their singing, their unbounded and unbinding inarticulation; for some humans lying is their calling, their bounded and binding articulation.

"Over time," I said, "humans listen to so many lies they start to think one lie matters the same as another."

In only two months Drummer and I would spend the day more or less entirely in bed. We would mightily fuck. Tenderly. Absurdly. I probably shouldn't have been thinking of the silver powder-down on the back of Drummer's neck as I held the two little ones, but I did, I thought of Drummer's soft barbs and barbicles at my fingertips. I thought of her knees, of the small depressions under her kneecaps, and I noted the segmentation of her leg, and in the moment of calling her leg to mind I called to mind the venation on female insects that have a place on the front of their legs with which to respond; their mechanoreceptors and proprioreceptors do not invite mere listening. They are sensitive sound organs. Excitable.

Drummer and I committed the lie of omission in which lovers will not speak the words.

It is January again. As we have done for over twelve years, when I see Drummer seventy-two days from now she will lie to me by not saying. I will lie to her in the same way.

The other was alert to me, to my breath. In the tent our breathing would often synchronize.

She had something to say. She looked at her sister, fast asleep. She wanted permission to say that she loved me. I would not grant that permission.

I continued my sage advice, so easily mocked. "One needs to listen to one's own lies and listen to other human lies. Actually listen — so you can discern. One should not judge until one actually listens. Some lies are forgivable. Some — a rare few — are not."

*

(No doubt you are wondering why this account of my Lie Advice is such a ridiculously shapedly lie. I often wish to sound Merlin-like — in a storybook way. Who doesn't?

I had mistakenly judged Carla to be one-dimensionally corrupt: a person who claimed power over the small miseries but none of the larger darknesses within her; who helplessly destroyed every fragile wonder in her own path. "Aggressive representation" is how she advertised her divorce law practice. In the community of Asheville she was an esteemed elder among her colleagues, who particularly admired her for being undetectably unethical.

As time has passed I have perceived that Carla could be depended upon to do the right thing as often as the wrong thing for her clients and for all of us. My understanding of this has been hard earned.

Elaine hired Carla to adjudicate the oddest parts of my parents' will. The choice of Carla made no sense to me. But you couldn't tell Elaine. You could not ever expect that she would hear.

A few years before my mother's death of cancer in 1993 and my father's death of unknown causes in 1997, they had asked that most of their savings go to a cause they believed to be dear to their two daughters: The National Treasure Tree Project.

Reading a bundle of my father and mother's letters exchanged during a period when they were in different hospitals, I have learned that they had contacted Carla about divorcing. My mother's illness was clearly fatal at that time; yet they were considering divorce, actually considering it very seriously. My mother wrote in one of her letters to my father:

We could go into the vault having left the vault — had we the courage. Do you agree? You should say you do if you do. Like this, my dear: "I do."

Carla expertly ensured that the will my father had finalized was "corrected" to split the funds between Elaine and me, with The Tree Project receiving the ridiculously small sum of fifty dollars semi-annually. Justice was done. So said my sister who seemed to sincerely think the new disbursement would please me.

When I was divorcing Robert, Carla murdered his spirit exactly as I asked. Already understanding that the process would diminish my own power in every regard, she motivated me to name for her the unspoken debts Robert owed me and others, every professional and personal shame that his unfaithfulness could possibly make him feel, every unanswered injury he had thoughtlessly inflicted upon me or others that I remembered from the past he had forgotten.

At my very first session with Carla, we agreed that my parents thought of Carla as another daughter. We talked about my family and the fifty-year friendship between Carla and Elaine and Robert and Robert's sister Amelia. This alliance, which had begun in grade school, had never included me.

Carla asked me about Robert's relationship to the members of his own family of origin. As his so-called friend, she already possessed much of this information. I should give my "version," she said, emphasizing that it was not important to be accurate; it was important that everything be convincing, believable to everyone, including Robert.

I obliged.

She took meticulous notes. If I had them, I would include them here.

For instance, I told her: Robert and his brother Tim had only recently recovered the loving relationship they had lost through Robert's neglect.

I told her that Robert had been close to his sister Amelia, but as an adult, Amelia came to love *me*; she came to love me as much or more than she did him.

Another piece of information: he was close to my sister Elaine, who came to love him as much or more than she did me.

Robert was close to his own father and mother, affected deeply by their divorce early in his life. He had been surprised by the force of that event, but, in any case, after decades of alienation from them, he had *shown* them *and told* them he loved each of them. This was a resolution he had made, and he had kept the resolution. At the very stage in his life when he broke his promise of faithfulness to me, all his other relationships brimmed with new promise and new vows of permanence.

I should have known — I did know — I did — what Carla would do with the information I fed her. She would turn and shape my words, as if on a lathe. Without much difficulty a practiced lawyer can make a divorce agreement wildly unjust.

In typed letters accompanying the proposed terms, she wrote to him that she strongly recommended an efficient divorce in order to restrict the time frame in which his friends and family members would learn about and respond to his adultery. She asked whether he had informed his colleagues at the elementary school. "Do they," she asked, "have any idea who you truly are?"

During each stage of negotiation she burned into him more shame about his affair by asking me to write him punishing letters. There in her office, coached at her giant polished steel conference desk, I wrote down variations on these words, which I understood were terribly truthful: Your father and mother would be ashamed of you, Robert. Your father and mother would understand that no ordinary divorce agreement can make this right.

From that desk, a shining paten, I left him long phone messages that would break him. The first words of the messages dared him, "Erase this, you coward . . ." and begged him, "Would you let me say what I need you to hear?" And bled him, "Do you want something from me — do you? — then listen . . ."

When I would mildly question the tactics, Carla would tell me his situation was laughable, that he had to live in his own shit, and it was pathetic that a man of his age cared at all what his father or mother thought.

These were cruelties I committed more easily as they compounded. I could live with them.

At any point that his sister might be bending toward showing Robert the smallest signs of compassion or understanding or, worst of all, support, Carla asked Amelia, younger than he, to say the truth to him, to write the truth to him, to say again how ashamed he should be. Amelia quickly understood that she should show no mercy in the processes of shaming and isolating him, threatening his livelihood in the community, demeaning him as a son and a husband and as her brother.

*

Their graymother delivered the two to me promptly at 3 PM, clothed appropriately and already fed, carrying in their small frame packs a week's supply of food for them and for me. Carla had brought filters for our water purifier. Of course she and the other grayparents paid for all my equipment, including the expensive purifying device.

Carla said she was glad to see me. I knew that she was. As far as she could determine, I was both a good and a questionable influence on her two children.

She had paid me in advance for the entire sonic adventure. At the beginning of each new month of the adventure, she would tip me for the previous one if she was pleased with her children's after-report. She gave me my tip check in a crisp new sealed envelope. Such generosity and calculation is hidden from children, and therefore it gives me pleasure to reveal the tip amount: $376. Each month, except for April and October when she offered no tip of any kind, she tipped Samantha Peabody that exact amount. Total tip amount: $3,384.

She asked me again about "the referral" she had made of three females, seven, six, and five, with a prosperous mother who was a "Greenie," a term she inflected with amused distance. Once more I explained that my sonic adventure enterprise, which was now focused entirely upon these two, would end in seven months and would never again resume.

I asked for a favor. "I would like that," I said, and pointed to her throat. She wore an expensive matte-black silk scarf, unusually long and light and almost sheer. The finely sewn single seam was glossy black. There were no tasseled ends. I do not like tassels, which are an affectation.

Without hesitation, she arranged the scarf around my neck, throwing one end over my shoulder where some of it pooled into the hood of my sweatshirt. She stepped back so that we could both look.

"I am so much like you," I said.

A pleased-startled person smiles a certain uncanny way. I could hear the sigh inside her smile. "Sam," she said. "Oh, Sam."

The three of us were groaning under our frame packs now. I said, "Unless we get lost we'll see you here in seven days."

She said to her daughters, "It will be only a week."

She said, "I will know."

As Carla drove away, the younger one began blurting out the story, explicitly disobeying her older sister. Carla had slapped the other hard enough that her ring ripped the child's cheek. It had been one episode; it really had been a single unprecedented event. They had been ordered to never tell.

The one said the other was lying. The other spat out the molten truth that only she, only she was slapped. Clearly, the injustice of that truth hurt her almost as much as the physical injury.

And then the two told me everything, including the efforts of Judge Warren to stop the slapping. And they told me that his photographs of her bruised and scabbed face were so vivid and he was so proud of the photos that he secretly showed them to the two.

And they told me about the break-up.

And they told me the mysterious details of Judge Warren's visits to their home during the last two weeks in January. And that made it possible for me to read between the lines that he was establishing the narrowly focused negotiating framework for systematic blackmail.

*

(You might now wish you had not told me all. Did you tell me all? And why would I include any of this? And why am I assembling this album for you in which I return the specimens of wonder and horror we observed together?

Tribute, I suppose.)

*

Before she drove away on that February afternoon, Carla held them for a long time, looking upon the involucrate leaves of their faces. She was trying to find the innermost leaves where the wonder of their love for their mother might be found, the wonder of her love for them. When the younger child was a newborn and the older child was two, Carla had effectively represented their birth mother in her divorce settlement. Less than a year later, their mother had drowned during a rafting trip on the French Broad River. Their father would not assume responsibility for them. When Carla saw that the two would become wards of the state, she had adopted them, surprising everyone who knew her, even surprising herself that she had made that choice.

*

(It was as if *you two chose her.*

If I am giving you certain pieces of information you have not had, I do not regret my incautiousness.)

*

Her arms around her two forms of surpassing awe, Carla said goodbye in the usual manner: "Don't get lost!"

On the trail, I said, "You are aware that I earn a handsome salary from you two?"

My statement made them laugh, which made their frame packs shift. I tightened the straps at their shoulders.

I sized them up, and I said, "By weight, height, and relative intelligence, I have placed you on a scale, and entered you in my automated cash register."

The one said, "Ka-ching!"

The other said, "Ka-ching!"

At the campsite, we inventoried. We stowed our water. We then carried the saltines, turkey jerky, and unsalted peanuts to the location of our bear canister. As they pulleyed the canister into the tree canopy, I said that I had trapped some shrews and meadow mice, and we would eat them tomorrow when the creatures had quit complaining so pitifully in their traps. The children knew, of course, that we would be eating saltines and turkey jerky and peanuts.

That evening, we heard great horned owls mating, a sound like a pillow fight in which there is crockery inside the feather pillows.

I asked whether there was more to say.

"It goes on a long time," said the other.

"The other birds don't like it," said the one, "they're making a lot of noise."

I asked, "Do you hear that they don't like it? Or do you assume that?"

"They are vocalizing," said the other. I was pleased that she used the appropriate term.

"They are responding," I said. "There are more of them this season, the mast season. They have enough food, so some have decided against heading south."

The owl racket continued. In their sleeping bags they had squeezed themselves against my bag. The half moon above us gave light traveling down through an icy wind.

I firmly took the outer whorls of their ears between my fingers and thumbs: the one's left ear, the other's right. I gave further instruction on the auricle. I said that I felt their ears would need to be slightly larger and less symmetrical for them to survive to adulthood. I explained to them about owl ears. On each side of the owl's head there are holes. The holes are not identical in shape, size, function. And this asymmetry assists the owl in locating prey in the dark — that is the theory. With one ear the owl reacts to the patterns of the familiar; with one ear the owl responds to the array of the unfamiliar. One ear directs attention; one ear decides the proportion of attention.

I asked if they would like their ears back, but I held them. I touched the gristly petals more gently. I said, "We're going into the fog tomorrow morning before sunrise in search of The Place of Nothing There. On our way we will pass through The Star Nests and we will listen for the winter timbre at Klingfarbe's Gorge. We will travel through Dog Hobble and Hell to the place of The Black Tongue."

This part of my shtick, except for The Black Tongue part, was well rehearsed. The sonic adventures always included this particular tightly plotted February excursion. The travelers and their leader easily got "lost" in search of The Place of Nothing There. This was specified in the sonic adventure contract I signed and the grayparents countersigned.

The one sputter-hummed in her sleep. When the moon shifted to a different drama in the forest's story, I pulled down my harp sling from its place behind my head. On the C harp I drew one note, my embouchure very soft. I lightly stopped my left ear with my thumb, and drew G-minor more quietly, and heard its acoustic location instantaneously move far inside me.

The other's open eyes were nacreous.

I almost completely stopped my left ear, and dropped my chin in order to sip the note from my lower lip. The sound took the form of the other.

"You have meteors in your eyes," I said.

She burrowed into her bag, hiding herself.

Through my left and right embouchure I drew notes of the tongue-stopped chord.

I said, "I met you when I was your age." I was glad for the mummified giggle my honest statement produced.

I did not say it to her then: I had met her in my first childhood moments in the secret garden. And I had never forgotten her: "When Mary Lennox was sent to Missellthwaite Manor to live with her uncle everybody said she was the most disagreeable-looking child ever seen. It was true, too."

A giggling lift of sound in her soft palate. Her breath shifting register.

Asleep.

Asleep.

*

I was grateful for the thick morning fog when we set out. The faces of the slopes had disappeared behind the fog but not the reverberating sounds of the waiting and the waited upon. Through the night I could hear the unlikely gentling sounds of a vulture keeping vigil near a dying creature. The creature, which sounded like an opossum, might have been a fox. The vulture would stay near, would not begin eating until its food was dead, and would not hurry the death along.

The two could identify the sound, but they did not wish to walk toward it in the unweaving darkness and mist. Still only half-awake, they held hands. They remained quiet so that they could hear. From one of the more isolated slope faces ahead came the bawl of coon dogs, English red ticks or black-and-tans, at a slick tree where scent had brought them to a dead end. The failed hunters blew their squallers, and the raccoon answered in a sporting chortle, then the calls of opossums and squirrels detonated inside their refuges.

The screams of wildcats, at a great distance from us, were immersive, that is, we moved inside their chilling sheaths and not away from or toward them. We shortened our strides, softened our footfalls, looked into each other's damp faces as if to ask, *Have you heard?* Water, moving water, river, river's changing pitch and timbre, breathing and beating, leaving and returning: this is the amniotic language to which our ears are tuned.

After his final stroke, Robert's breathing had shifted in tempo, in pitch, in depth. Elaine was there, and she gave me her account. His brother Tim visited, but he left and did not return. Amelia felt she would be disloyal to me if she visited him, and so she did not go until the very end when she and Elaine heard his last words.

They did not tell me. I asked, and they did not tell me. It would be July 2004 before I would learn his last words.

I remember that in the final stages of the divorce agreement, Robert had asked for his copy of *The Secret Garden,* a volume over sixty years old. His father's name, William H. Peabody, was handwritten in the upper right-hand corner of the flyleaf. William had read to him from his very first day of life, had read this one copy to him many times. His mother Julia had read his favorite chapters to him during the year before he could read it himself, claiming the book for his own room. Mary and Dickon and Colin were as real to Robert as any of his childhood friends. Robert had been inordinately happy that *The Secret Garden* also profoundly affected me as a child.

I kept his library. Carla strongly recommended that I keep the librarian's library, every book: "a punch to the Adam's apple," she called the plan.

On the day she acquired his signature on the divorce agreement, I considered giving him the book he'd requested. Instead, I had her give him a fancy Barnes & Noble copy of *The Secret Garden* that he had lovingly inscribed for me in the first wonderful year of our marriage, "The two of us in the secret garden. A miracle, Sam. A miracle."

On the next part of our trail, the mist changed in movement and color. We walked through a field of Queen Anne's lace, and the plants' high starry nests brushed dew onto us. Through this fog a straight row of trees grew from a nurse log, a decayed fallen tree from which tree seedlings have grown; they almost looked as if a farmer had carefully planted them. Together, we silently counted the trees: twelve. We were wearing our green gloves, our green socks; only for that moment, our hoods were closed tight over our heads and snapped closed under our chins. The other wore the black scarf her mother had given me. The three of us were well muffled in our layers, including long underwear, but the cold wind's long proboscises reached in, and since our effort to be absolutely quiet had cooled us down, we were not too happy to hear the fountains of cold air gushing upward from the place ahead.

I took smaller steps, and my two students did the same. The whooshing plumes of freezing air had fine, reflective particulate in them, mica and leaf litter and exploded pollen sacks and molted flight feathers. Fragrances and rank odors shot up and dispersed so high they were scrubbed to their essences by the time we breathed them in.

The inner maw of the gorge was ringed in gray-velvet descending fog; the outer golden ring of ascending fog was made dense by the sunrise's full signal.

The idea now was to walk so slowly toward Klingfarbe's Gorge that we could take in the sounds in the far and near orbit of the gorge's strange founts of up-rushing air. I had explained to them that this deliberate stride was the way for us to be penetrated by the radial zones of sound there. I wished for them to learn a different habit than the usual habit of ignoring how sound radiates through us and surrounds us.

The two walked slow-footed and alert. They unsnapped their chin straps. They were trying very hard to hear nature's resonances converging; they wished to be penetrated by the one great reverberating presence that causes affinity with the All.

How do I know this?

I don't. I don't. It is a prayer I made up. I find myself making up the prayer again each time I enter another item in this album.

We pulled back our earflaps. We progressed approximately two feet for each three minutes toward the orchestral center. We did not speak, though we looked into each other's eyes often. I interposed so that I could have my hands inside theirs. The one's stomach burbled. The other's stomach burbled, as if in response.

The two understood that smiles would have been unacceptable.

We heard planets and major and minor moons of sound. We heard churnings of sound, and eruptions and meteor bombings and comet tails of sound. We heard our imaginations making some of the sounds into music and some few into noise.

A little less than two hours later, at about 8:45, we were at the maw. I let their hands go, but I kept them close. By this time, our ears were gorges hearing the gorge hear itself.

We had not noticed the disappearance of the rings of fog, and so we were dangerously close to the gorge's southern exposure. We could have easily stepped off and fallen hundreds of feet.

We glanced down. I closed my eyes in order to silently command the children to close theirs and to *listen down*. I held my hands on their shoulders. Their eyes were not clamped shut; they were lightly closed upon the gorge's sonic pleasures.

I moved my fingers on their slender necks: fa — so — la.

I pulled them back from their impulse to make the dreamer's dive. I whispered the first words spoken in hours: "Let's not die today."

There was a safe ledge a few yards from us, a good place to sit with our legs dangling and have the sensation of them dangling from the lip of the void.

The gorge did not at all constantly blow, though that is how it seemed. The other said, "That's pretty far down."

"Duh," said her sister.

The one's eyeglasses were in need of cleaning, so I took them from her face, handed her my gloves, and polished them with my shirttail. I put them on her face again. She and the other: how would they ever know that my connection to them on that day was, deep in the spirit, more pure than I had ever experienced? I felt convergent with them. Okay, yes, I offered another prayer. I prayed more than any scientist should; no wonder that my highest achievement as a scientist was to become the leader of sonic adventures for children, for ill-prepared little things whose graymothers needed relief.

But there is this: In the years I have been apart from the two, I have truly known purity of love for the woods around me only when I have remembered to receive the transmissions of the infinite worlds here with the intensity and precision and presence with which the two would hear.

"Your frames are crooked," I said.

I asked the other, "You've brought the scarf?" I had not told her why we'd brought it.

"Hand it to me."

To glory in being its exclusive keeper, she held it tightly in her green fists.

I explained that at the right moment she was going to throw it into the gorge as an offering. I forewarned them that the scarf might fly back to us and call out to us, "Whish-whishwhiiiiiish!" and fall back from us, "Whish!" and I warned the two against trying to reach for it.

I ordered them to sit and to let the scarf come to them — if that was meant to be.

I said, "We are waiting for northwest wind to hit the flume of the rock walls. This is quite exactly the time of year and the right weather conditions, and the perfect time of day."

The one said, "I'm scared."

"Duh," I said.

"Duh," said the other.

Something writhed in the stillness of the gorge floor.

I shook my head *no* so the two could clearly see my gesture; and when the something grunted, I gave the other the not-yet signal. A witch's ladle stirs Klingfarbe's Gorge, the old people say. Her gown is gold, alive as webworm shrouds. Some of them have seen flutterings far inside the fog, and they have called her Mother Covey. Some who remember their father's great-grandfather's memories of flintlock smoke call her Flint Mist. When you see her, they tell you, it is already too late.

The children gazed at me to know they were all right. They looked at each other to erase doubt.

We heard up-wickings, up-sputterings, up-twistings coming from far below where an inverted tornado whirligigged and whisked. The Silvershawl, who has worn the fog for eons, dresses and undresses there, say the old ones.

When we suddenly heard the whirlwind change in volume from blast to after-blast, I commanded the other to throw the scarf high and directly in front of her.

The propulsive tongue of air searched with a slurping sound, lengthened and strained to lengthen more — *thit! thit!* It torqued, licked up the scarf from over our heads, tasted our scalps.

The gorge swallowed the fine black tail.

Our faint flames of laughter were extinguished upon hearing the scarf kiting down there — whithit whithit whithit — before the slight band of fabric corkscrewed back into our sight and up at least twenty feet above the gorge — *whish-whish whiiiiiiish* — but not within our grasp — *whish-whish whiiiiiish* — then within our grasp, then not, then within if we would follow and plunge down — *whish!* — and, without moving from our ledge, we vibrated against each other like scales of cliff-slate beginning to give way.

The vertical drilling brilliance became horizontal in an instant.

*

(A copy of my will is in Drummer's possession. She and I are not growing younger; at the appropriate time, you may request the scarf from her.)

*

The black cloth floated down upon my shoulders, and stayed silent.

"Sam Peabody," the gorge called.

"Sam Peabody!" I echoed back.

"Would you," I asked, "like to see Drummer's cabin?"

*

All approaches to her cabin, which was not far from the gorge, were mined with dog hobble and rhododendron hells. One cannot step into that maze without twisting an ankle or falling and wrenching your arms. They call the rhododendron thickets "hells" because each one is a different kind of perfect grave. Old bears, who have chosen their dens and their hunting grounds well, will chase prey into the hobbles and the hells, where snakes also rest and wait.

There are visual illusions of escape possibilities as you enter a hell, and the first steps for some reason increase the illusions, until steps backward or to the side cannot be made, until the mesh and the web of roots and low branches fix you with many tight shoes and ankle chains. If you bend over too far or get down on all fours in order to re-balance, you pay dearly for your bad choice.

In the hill stories, ripe blackberries and raspberries and paw paw grow there. The special labor that has chosen people also names them and theirs: Sapper, Cobbler, Shiner, Parson's Oldest, Hod's Boy, Sharp's Wild Card. You grow into the stories of the teeming place.

And greedy children who don't work hard enough grow there. They envy the blackberries and raspberries and paw paw and red sumac berries that are the lean children's harvest tasks.

The children who do not work hard enough are unproductive children. They're selfish children who want to go in under the friendly sunlight. They're secretive because they want the berries for themselves. They are unprepared.

A dozen steps past the hobble into the hells, their gluttony has made them almost sick under the burning sun.

They crawl beneath the branches and they curl up like thousand-leggers. And when they wake under the glittering edge of the sun, a net of shadow has been thrown over everything. The slender ropy branches restrict with any pull against them.

In the afternoon, beetles and ants investigate the cool insides of the lazy children's socks and their pants legs. In some of the stories a bright orange eft with red spots and a long speaking tail arrives. The tail whips left, whips right, asks, "How long? How long?"

The tale of the eft is a long tale, of course. The eft has a long path from being a land eft to eventually becoming a newt in a pond. It has traveled a long path from the first pond where it was once a tadpole, brown, and with gills.

Evening comes under the sun's last seethings.

The children call for help, but they were never hardworking, good children.

And a season passes before the mother and father notice less food goes to and from the table.

It is often winter at the end of these stories, usually a heavy winter. And when all the snow has melted, the thirsty mantles of rhodo and hobble growth have drunk their fill and have stretched their fingers and limbs, and have become impenetrable.

Sometimes a grandmother will want the little body found. Dead honeysuckle or kudzu has streamered every part of the freakish decaying cemetery the child should never have entered when it was so resplendently green.

But the grandmother. She has made herself heard: Find the little body.

All of it, all of it covering the wasted little human-fruit must be burned.

The dead shroud is set on fire by young, excited fire-setters who have been given fistfuls of splinters. The youngest of them provides the flaming punk.

A low-burning fire's flames lick downward.

Old heads of rank smoke rise from the bed. They offer warnings to all bad, greedy children. The small and graceful heads coming later also offer warnings to them, to the selfish, unprepared children who do not work hard.

A charcoal the shape of a bad child will be found and buried.

Or: If no fire is set, the goats must be loosed on it, and they will eat down to the dirt, and drag out the skeleton in the shape of a foolish child who will be forever left under the demon sun.

I pointed to the small cabin and said, "You can't get there without crawling."

The one said she was hungry, that she didn't see the cabin.

The other said, "You know the way?"

"You're my scouts," I said, "you go in." I was standing in a specific location familiar to me through many years of March and

September meetings with Drummer and through many sonic expeditions.

"But. I don't even see it," said the one.

"Me neither," said the other.

"Listen," I said, "remember that when raccoons go in there they are food for the snakes; chickens go in there and they are food for the foxes; the foxes go in there and they're there for the wildcats." I did not say that the coyote watches the whole parade and howls with laughter. I did not say that the coyote knows the way in there and, like Drummer and Samantha Peabody, knows the way out.

Nearly one hour later, the children, a little scratched up, more than a little frightened but in control of their fear, made it through. I had called directions to them from my special tree perch close to but not in sight of Drummer's cabin.

On all fours, their shoulders bunched, their teeth bared in anger, they could not see me as I could see them.

They called out, "Pea!"

I said, "I'm here."

They were almost out. Almost free. The younger crouched down. The older crouched down, too. Like previous sonic adventurers, they should have felt abandoned, terrified.

Not these two.

They called out, "Pea!" and called out again.

They were not at all surprised when I said, "I'm up here on a tree above you. You have two more feet to crawl. Bear right."

We then sat under my observation tree and ate the little meal I had packed for us. A jug band of a dozen birdhouse gourds lit and rekindled and let the last air out of three bars of song. I pointed at Drummer's place where wind set off the gourd-band again. Her cabin was there behind a natural berm, under dense successions of cove hardwood and in a depression that was out of fog for only a few hours a day in January and February.

They still could not see the cabin. They did not believe me.

They were sure nothing was there.

". . . who will forever be left under the demon sun."

The two had asked me to tell them again about the children who would not work hard.

Not all sonic adventurers wished to hear the story, though I always offered: a fine story with many rattling branches and with erratic silences, the swallowing-down and sucking-in silences.

I asked if they were awake.

They were.

When the story had arrived at the lighting of the fires I asked if I should go on, and I was given their approval. When the story introduced the goats, I took their non-responses as further approval. The spring foliage around and above our campsite muted certain distant sounds and encapsulated us as if we were silky chestnuts. The senses fuse when one is held in the rose-velvet lining that is contained in the prickly bur of a very cold March. The sound and soundlessness inside our tent was isolating, it was pungent, tightening our scalps, reissuing cidery and sour tastes in our mouths.

The one asked if I would play, and the other said, "You should play something good."

"I will not take that personally," I said.

They shrugged inside their flesh in a certain way. My flesh was attuned. They didn't shiver, but I could feel they were cold. "Come in here with me."

They shed their sleeping bags and entered mine. When they found their accustomed positions, I wiped down my B♭ harp. I cleaned the reeds with an unused mascara brush Drummer had provided me. I admire the sophisticated camouflage of mascara, though personally I have never had need of it to blend into my surroundings.

I played "When My Mama Was Living." I'd listened endlessly to Louisiana Red sing in his hoarse young-owl hungering cry that gave six hoots to the word *When* before the six notes of *my mama was living*. On the long draws I tried to sink the knife into the middle octave, but hardly drew blood. I had taught them about distinguishing hyperlocalized and delocalized sounds: how the harp more or less accurately transmitted the sounds of my breath, but how the taking-flight sounds in the woods were often landing sounds in actuality; how the sound source is apprehended and how easily it is misapprehended.

✳

(Twelve years later, do you remember any of what I taught you?

And why do I care?

I suppose my album is the manual, the test, the itemized bill I bring.)

*

I sang the song in the manner Louisiana Red would sing but softer, a version that was too soft and did not bring in the acid of his hurt: "When my mama was living, I was loved just because of me. / When my mama was living, I was loved just because of me."

I sang softer yet; I softly sang into the harp. I sounded "luuuu-UHvd" from one note bent with a dwah of my tongue and lips, and then a sheeshing five-note chord reduced to a three-note chord swallowed hard and choked. I played two hard-throttled head-shake quiet, quiet notes. I worked on those two falterings for half an hour or more.

They fell asleep hard. And that gave me the opportunity to un-zip my bag, to unpackage my hidden tube of *BodyBaby!*, to go outside, to "water the plants" as my delicate sister Elaine would say, along with at least a thousand things more that she would compulsively add.

I pulled off my cotton briefs and left them inside. I wished to avoid infesting our tent with the Asian needle ants that were a new invasive species in the Pisgah Range. One of my sonic adventurers in the past had been stung painfully by *Pachycon-dyla chinensis*. As with many insects, its choral singing repels and attracts by sounding only the tone-tail of what a human might think is a word: "— *en* — *en* — *en*."

At the latrine, without need of a flashlight, I found the low, slender branch-seat that was mine, I braced myself, and I leaned back. I could hear the rust-scraping chewing noises of the pine sawyers. I could hear the soirée of earthworms dancing leaf rubbish and twig-trash into their burrows. When one has accepted that it is not impossible to hear the earthworms, one does hear: the worm families, the irrepressible din of the neighborhoods, the communities and counties and regions and kingdoms of worms. A long friendship with a single earthworm is possible because one worm can live for fifteen years. Yet this kind of friendship is not probable, and I do not feel sadness about that fact.

When I stood up, I applied *BodyBaby!* to my legs and feet. A combination of faintly scented body lotion and baby oil, it caused a sheen which had once enticed Robert. I would stand before him wearing nothing but that luster, and I could hear the pattern of his breathing syncopate. If, out of the blue — in the library, on a bus, at the tax office — my lips touched the lobe of his ear as I whispered, *"BodyBaby!"* he howled with — and hardened with — pleasure and excited delight.

If Robert and I were camping, and I left the tent at night, I would hear his grunt of laughter. When I returned, he would not ask. We would hold each other, and sometimes I would rub my lubricity into the dry skin of his hairy legs, and we would laugh together at our habits of letting loose.

Until now I had disclosed this secret camping pleasure to no one.

I paced outside the tent until the frigid air stung. I wished for it to hurt me.

"One worm," I said to the two, as I fitted myself again between them, "can have forty thousand young."

In the morning, as we were dressing, we heard the reedy mantras of sadhu redwings, we heard shrews twittering, and there was something else, a buzzing noise one usually only hears in late March.

"Have you heard?" I asked.

The younger said, "Forty thousand?"

The older asked, "Pea. Forty thousand what?"

I explained about our friends the earthworms. I also explained that an earthworm is both female and male, and cross-fertilizes toe to head.

I asked, "But what is the buzzing noise in our campsite? If one of you can tell me what the buzzing noise is I will not eat your portions of our crackers later today."

❊

At our meal, in order to cement the sonic lesson, I ate their crackers and identified for them the calling spiders. I had collected one for us to listen to, and the very instant I brought her out of the medicine bottle, she indignantly vibrated her papillae. *Zbizz-zbizzzz.*

I released her.

I was not being fair to the two, since I had never told them anything about calling spiders. I gave them a little of my turkey jerky.

We set out to audio-locate broods, not easy to do in daylight even in this season of active mating and brooding. I had never trained more sensitive scouts than these two, who had begun to absorb life and, in particular, life's periodicity. They were my two owl ears, and through them I heard the abundances and absences in the air, on the high and low branches, in the hollow trunks, on the creek beds and banks, along the ground, inside and at the entrances to the animal and insect burrows.

More of Carla's story had found me regarding their mother and Judge Warren. Elaine had sent me the recent newspaper clippings. *The Asheville Citizen-Times* had reported that Carla Tieck-McClary, Board Certified Specialist in Family Law, was under investigation for charges not yet made public. Local authorities were involved, and a North Carolina Bar Association spokesperson had confirmed that the charges were "too serious to ignore." I could complete the newspaper's incomplete story: all of this meant that War had sent her a warning shot; he could give the paper more at any time. It meant that her daughters would be interviewed, that associates such as Samantha Peabody might be sought out. And soon enough, if she did not concede to be blackmailed by War, his photos of "the battered child" would be reprinted in the local paper.

We had walked up-creek to a small rock-fall meadow, a place of stillness because one feels the earth's imminences there among the mossing boulders and snapped trunks and the naked root clods. Forgetting the goal of hearing brooding sounds, I asked if we had the materials for them to show me new dance moves.

Starting in December, whenever they taught me new moves, we would grab small fallen pine branches for the dance. Each of us would have eleven pairs of protruding appendages (in our fists, up our sleeves, stuffed into our shoes) for propelling ourselves in any direction. We would imitate one of Samantha Peabody's favorite specimens: the fairy shrimp. We would dance as true phyllopods do.

"I don't feel like it," said the older one.

"Me neither," said the younger.

I asked whether their mother had told them about what was happening with Judge Warren.

My blunt question caused the other to stagger as if I had swung a branch at her ankles. She reached out helplessly, and the one let her lean into her.

And they actually pretended that nothing had happened.

Humans are untrue.

Humans lie.

A child of six, a child of eight: with alarming speed a child will perfect the practice of dishonesty. When Elaine was approximately that age, she flushed my mother's chicken almond casserole down the toilet, then told her that I, who had always proclaimed my hatred of the casserole, had thrown the food away in the backyard. She put the gooey empty pyrex dish in the part of the garden that was my special place. She was so convincing that for an instant — exactly the wrong instant under my mother's scrutiny — I believed I must have committed the crime. I said, "I really, really, really hate casserole," and then, "but —"

The one said, "I hear something. There's something   like when you brush against a tinkly wind chime." The other said,

"Birds, huh?" The one said, "There's something in the nests."

"Something in the squirrels' nests," said the other, and I was pleased that she was alert to the newly built nests of the red squirrels where the young would soon appear.

"There's always something in *some* of the nests," I said. I wanted them to know I wasn't so easily distracted from the topic at hand, so easily played. "Nests," I said, "will fool you because they are everywhere."

The percussion section was tuning up: the drumming male ruffed grouse and the loud talon-scratchings of the fox sparrow. The grackles were thug-chattering against the singing of brown-headed cowbirds and busy robins. Some nests were abandoned and some had only been decoy nests after all and had become crash pads for wasps.

I wished to say more. I had their mother in my thoughts, and that means I had Robert in my thoughts; along with Robert came his sister Amelia, and along with Amelia, Elaine; along with Elaine came my husband's unidentified lover; along with all of them the Samantha Peabody I had convinced myself I had once been, blameless Sam, betrayed Sam, vengeful and re-venged Sam.

I wished for them to say more. They wanted to know if I heard.

The sound was behind us, and the hem of a March *derecho* swept it toward us. We held still in order to let the wind-sound gain on us.

The one concentrated by looking down; the other followed her lead. I could see them blocking visual stimuli but I could also see them looking far, far down together into a void.

Several cawings formed clipped sounds of compellation. In the next moment, I felt the two fully taking in the wallop of this child-storm of cawing, and taking in their own graymother-cyclone memories, and utterly failing to concentrate upon present or past.

"I am not going to touch you, or hug you," I said. "You do not want that."

✻

(You did not want that.

Did you want that?)

✻

"I know where the sounds are," I said. "We'll go to them." I already knew the source of the sound would further sadden the children, and would also begin curing their sadness. I had faith then — I have it now — in counter-extinguishing sorrows.

We walked and aimed wrong and walked and aimed, quieting ourselves and becoming more aware of the stain in the source of the sounds.

There was no sentinel crow there to give warning.

There was no flock to creak-caw or to crack-caw or to bash the air all at once with hundreds of alarm-sounding wings.

No black male or identically black female circled over the nest or landed on the nest-edge to bark-caw at the two little hungering storms.

The one touched her binocular case. I nodded that she could go ahead and use the binoculars. She seemed to ask permission from the other, who did not give it. I had taught them to hear by subtracting sight. I had taught them to visualize internally (with restraint) but not to allow the distraction of external visualization. I had taught them discipline and I had taught them co-discipline.

For half an hour we stood under the tulip tree where the young brood of crows was sputtering and spitting and laugh-cawing at the long wait of dying. When birds mate too soon and the conditions are not right for the brood to stay warm, they do not survive. Chance is always involved in admission to life. To become food for the birds, the tent caterpillars must have months of cold and the deep sleep of diapause to become moths. So much is dying above us, calling from a supernal grave.

On the walk back, the other said, plainly, flatly: "We're moving away." She walked ahead of us a step, and pivoted back to us.

"A good neighborhood?" I asked.

The one said, "Not far away from our house."

"Not the same school, not our school," said the other from behind us.

Their school was important to them. When they talked about their teachers, the tone of their speech enriched in intensity. I have heard that tone coming from inside a hen's eggs when the hen knocks on the shells, nudges them with her beak in order to center them in their suspended states. She will do this every hour until the chicks first begin to hatch.

I wanted to relieve the pressure on the two, but I needed to know. "What about April?" I was aware I sounded five years old.

They said that their mother had told them they would go on the April adventure, no matter what. I was relieved so greatly that I felt the breath go out of me. "She has paid me in advance," I said, "You do not have to be concerned for me."

The other spoke for herself and for the one: "We're not."

When the clouds unfastened, the stream flashed sun-brightness as if asking for us to hear each other's gasp when we saw at our feet the red trillium. I am certain they remember: we actually gasped, our breaths taken away by the wake robin trillium that had appeared in the same instant as our sadness about the two of them moving away, about losing their school, about the outcomes of their graymother's choices.

I remember thinking that it must have been Carla's strategy to accept loss on this battlefront while looking beyond it to the next. I believed she had pretended absolute helplessness about the inevitable loss of her law practice; I believed that in slow increments and then in brutally fast attacks she would sink her formidable knives into War, repeatedly wound him in very public, lethal ways. The legal butchery she had mastered, the methods of violation: this judge, who had simply never applied himself to that set of skills with Carla's absolute dedication, would learn a lesson in human justice. I was certain.

What she ultimately chose to do: I could never have guessed.

✳

In the early evening, we purified our water, filling our bottles all the way to the top. Our drip-purifying devices made the daily procedure easy. Our one-liter collection bottles were clear plastic. The dimpled bottom of the bottle formed a kind of eye and iris. We sat near each other on the creek bank, our bare feet dangling in at the pooling place near our campsite. We each gazed into the wide-mouth clear cap of our bottles, and we looked through at the dissolving appearances of things reflected upon the creek's surface and distorted by the imperfect lens. I saw a webbed branch of new leaves closed and shaking their ghost-fists; and inside the fists jetting poorwills snared flying jewels. I thought, *This is chill!*

I saw in the river the bifacial one and other. In their glasses and in their eight lenses the circle of their lashes closed and opened over magmatic forms.

For humans to have the compound eye that connects and does not categorize would be a great disadvantage. And a great advantage.

The one squinted at me through her telescopic bottle. Through mine I saw her, her claws holding in front of her the spilling goblet of her own child-cocktail-glass arthropodal head. She asked, "Will you be gone tonight?"

I said that it was my night with Drummer but that I would be back with them at sunrise the next day.

"Only one night," said the other.

"Why only one night?" asked the one.

"In fact, I'll have more than one night since I'll see her again in September. We are lovers. The *two* nights together are important to us."

We were walking now toward our latrine which was approximately six hundred yards up-creek from our camp. Systematizing latrine maintenance was part of the adventure training.

"But."

"I've told you enough."

"But."

"The two nights are what Drummer and I want."

The other and the one were alert. At that moment, in order to assert their awareness, in order to check me in my lie about the sufficiency of the two nights, they asked each other, "Have you heard?"

I said that I was not misinforming them about my relationship with Drummer. Now I'm struggling to remember the words I used because, I supposed, I do not like to remember verbatim my untruths.

"She's older than you?" the other asked.

"A lot older?" asked her sister.

I said, "Older by ten years." I thought, Drummer is as old as the first order of angels.

That order of angels is called "The Seraphs." Recapturing the exact term matters to me. I do not summon only words native to my hearing; I do not apologize for singing the accidental and rare accidental word-sounds, the vagrants and rare vagrants.

The word-sounds leave. One recalls them for a moment, and they leave.

*

(Do you see?

I want them back.)

*

I remember asking the two whether the shitty smell of our latrine was too strongly shitty.

"Strong enough," said the one.

We had come to a moss-covered nurse log like the log we had encountered on our expedition to Klingfarbe's Gorge. A nurse log always draws my attention. I have recently determined that this particular old nurse log was approximately sixty-six years old at that time.

The two climbed up onto it and threaded their way through the three-meter yellow birches that seemed to have moved in measured paces over the log and then to have stopped and sent medusa roots through the trunk and over the sides. In the future when the nurse log had completely dissolved, there would be this perfect alignment defying comprehension, there would be these elegant yellow birches en pointe.

The two were happy for me that I would be with Drummer. They felt delight that they had pulled from me that thread of my own knot of secrets.

*

When I left the tent, the kind of rain was falling that the Chero-
kee call "walking rain" for how its pale, swaying and sweeping
robes appear when seen on a distant ridge to be the clothing of
ancients walking through the mountains.

"Sam Peabody," whispered Flint Mist. "Sam Pea Sambodysam
Peasam Peabody," sang the sunrise light staggered by the trees
and bushes in the mist.

I stopped sometimes and closed my eyes and listened. I heard.
A guzzling, a gasping. The soft but wild singing of my name,
somepeabody somepeabuddy somesambawdy.

And why didn't she take my hand and walk with me to her
cabin? Why did she stay in the mist and call my name through
the rain?

Is it more powerful to be seduced by a sound from a distance?
Does the distance make you feel that what sings *to* you is
singing *from* you in the same moment?

How do you account for someone as strange as Drummer?

Factor in that she was already stumbling-down drunk.

This was March 2004. Male rufous hummingbirds had arrived for the breeding season, and they had found Drummer's
small acoustical niche. In October they would return to their
wintering lands, subtracting from the Pisgah soundscape
their infrasonic pulses, sounds without destination or apparent source. The sounds surround instead of direct me, I must
go inward to "hear" where and when they began in me, when
and where they ended in me. I prehend the first high- and low-
pitched notes of wings, tail, ecstatic body. The sound does not

travel toward me. It is *of* me. How will we human travelers find our true natures when our hummingbird guides have gone from the air?

٭

I had felt excited anticipation about my visit to Drummer.

Until I reached her cabin door she would walk near me but in the mist.

At the door she would stand very straight, look directly at me, not letting me look away. I would feel her cold shawl enclose me, and her cold arms. Her cold cheek would press against mine, and, while we kissed, the key would resist, as ever, and I would have to withdraw it one notch and give it a strong lift up while turning it right in order to tumble the mechanism open.

On the bedside table would be two large bottles of her own formula for Jamaica Ginger Shine. There is no comparable aphrodisiac. It is only a few ingredients different than the Jamaica Ginger Formula that in 1930 caused fifty thousand people in the South to have "jake-leg" and half that number to be permanently disabled.

We would fuck each other in her cabin, fall into a thrashing-in-the-flesh-stoned-burning-gut silence, fuck each other some more, pull on clothes and smoke cigarettes — always damp cigarettes in March, always Wythe County weed in September — and she would ask about the difficulties of my self-deliverance, and I would ask about her own. We would agree that in the forest's dark depths you should make no effort on the path, and, better yet, you should have no path.

We would fuck some more but then fuck around as opposed to fuck because by that time it would be impossible to find our mouths with our bottles, our mouths with our mouths, our fingers with our tongues.

That afternoon Drummer gave me letters from Elaine. Long letters.

Elaine wrote that there was something she wished to tell me but she would not write it, she had to say it to my face. I should let her visit frequently, she wrote, and "Why not, Sam? You act like I've done something wrong." She wrote that she should have had children when she could have. Cribs and baby carriages and birthday celebrations. She went off on the baby imperative. The letters asked if I thought she would have been a good mother. She speculated about how difficult and marvelous — more difficult than marvelous — her children would find their Aunt Sam.

She asked whether I thought she could be a good "graymother." She told me she felt the term was demeaning, that designations were not names and that even a grayscientist should understand that.

My visit with Drummer was more exciting and fulfilling than I could have imagined. Always true then. True now.

In the evening Drummer brushed my really short hair, which means she gave my scalp a delicious scoring. She asked me if I would talk to her about the two. I was thankful to her for asking, because they crowded my heart and claimed it so beautiful-terrible much.

✳

(My dear ones, I worry that I create confusion for you as you read this. Did you believe you would be the central concern of my album? Or that these pages would give more attention to Drummer and Robert and Carla and everyone else than to the sonic contours of this forest where I stir and am stirred?

Can you accept that you two who matter like life and death to me do not matter more than the voice of the Pisgah?)

*

Drummer and I sucked one cigarette down between us, and sucked another and another, and the moonshine made us sweat and gave us gooseflesh, so we pulled the bedcovers over us and smoked and drank there. I told her more, since the drink made me. I warmed her troubled left foot in my hands, and I could feel the tremulations of old healing in the bones there and of older pain, and I realized there was no end to how long I could talk about the two. All night, I called them My Sweet Two.

At various times in the night one or the other of us had a bolting back spasm, then fainted hard, and a few minutes later we came to in each other's arms. We did not blather about love, because Drummer and I knew we wished to not speak about that, we wished to love apart and not together.

Though there was gagging and heaving and lung-tearing coughing, there was no vomiting — not yet — because this was the kind of moonshine causing every small and large opening of the body to convulse almost exactly twenty-four hours after the first dose. I knew I would be in bad shape on the next day of the sonic adventure.

I hurried back to them. I fairly ran back to them, stumbling and muttering to myself.

I have reflected on this part of the album; at times, I have obsessed over this part.

*

(Here is a question I must ask. If you two have given me the benefit of the doubt as you've read this, you must ask: Did Samantha Peabody really leave two small children — someone else's children entrusted to her care — alone in the woods for so many hours? Was she a person with no integrity whatsoever? Was she one hundred times more reprehensible than a graymother who slapped a child hard enough to bruise her?)

*

At camp, My Sweet Two were fine, asleep and clutching each other's hands. They must have felt confident I would return exactly when I promised.

They had wondered if they could ever know more about Drummer and me, of that I have no doubt.

And now they will know.

April 2 – 8, 2004

The early morning sleet storm moved with accelerating speed from south to north through the woods, a raging-fire sound. Having compensated for frequency, I would now estimate its relative loudness as somewhere between 64.0 and 128.0 sones. Townsend-Hendrix-Marshall-stacked-amps loud.

"Should I do this?" Inside her car, a Lexus IS F Sport, the graymother of the two had not taken down her absurdly large raincoat hood, and she seemed to ask the question from the aperture of a gastropod shell.

I answered, "You mean, should you leave them with me, Carla?" Quite possibly, she had asked me another kind of question, but I chose the one to which I would respond.

"Aren't they safer with me — than you?" I asked. I knew there had been only the one incident in which she had hurt the other. It had not happened again, not at all. I knew that. I believed that.

Behind me were the two, already bowed under the burden of their full backpacks.

They had said their goodbyes and, with their backs to her, they were looking into the refracted zephyrs of sunlight — and they were listening.

She had noticed that they were not wearing their rain gear, and she asked me why.

"They have their rain jackets in their backpacks," I said.

"But they're not wearing them."

She tried to look past me to them. I blocked her. "Here is a riddle," I said. "When is a rain jacket only A Good Read?"

"I don't know, Sam. I don't like riddles."

"You like verdicts."

"I like verdicts."

"Some day, ask them for the answer to the riddle. They will know exactly to what you are referring."

"This is not a good storm."

"This is a moving storm," I said.

I was frustrated that I was unable to discern where the storm would be moving next. In a sleet storm when glass shards of ice scalpel through the green tissues of broadleaf forest, a Doppler effect results, altering every kind of calculation.

I got inside the car, and I sat with her. Sometimes one has no choice but to be compassionate for a brief moment.

Looking out at the two, she asked nothing. I liked being asked nothing, I preferred conversation with her in which nothing proceeded. I could have asked whether their new apartment was suiting her and the children, whether the new school presented unforeseen problems. I could have asked whether Warren was still in their lives; I had a suspicion he had not left them alone.

I answered her nonquestion: "I am taking them to a pillow-and-cradle site, a one-kilometer walk from our camp."

"In this weather?"

"If necessary," I said. "After all, I have an instruction plan." I did not say exactly what my instruction would include. Weaponry training is not listed in the Sonic Adventure information materials; until these two, I had never included such training in my lesson plans.

She did not know what to do with her hands. She rested them on the driver's wheel. Her nails were manicured, her favorite shellac color, Hot Chilis. She said, "The sun is out — it's sleeting and the sun is out."

She did not ask me to explain the pillow-and-cradle phenomenon. I said, "We're going to a place that is an impossibility, a wondrous place to be lost. Have you ever seen those old post-hurricane pictures of a perfectly fine vinyl LP driven halfway through a telephone pole?"

"Huh?" she asked.

"It's a place like that."

She did not know what to do with her body, and she shifted herself into greater discomfort. She did not know what to do with her feet. She lightly poked the car mat with her heels. A seventy-two-year-old professional wearing nylons and stiletto heels: an unlovely hatchery trout.

I listened to her spindly breathing.

She wished to be held.

She would have appreciated a kind word.

I said, "I should go," and I thanked her for bringing along the three pints of fruit juice I had requested.

"You never let me bring juice before," she said, a lawyerly observation.

"Water is best out here."

"They'll enjoy it," she said.

I answered, "I believe they will."

"They look cold. Even bundled up."

"They *are* cold," I said.

This graymother of the two was someone a human being would remember from the first moment. The greater the degree to which any particular creature is benign, the more forgettable that creature is at all points in time; since the outermost neural warning systems detect no threat, they send no beware-of-me signal. If the creature is far from benign, it matters how far, since the threat is proportional to the danger, and the brain attends. In every shabby small space and pristine grand room of the vast storehouse of memory, the brain is alert to someone like Carla. A warning penetrates: She might be near.

I remember that after my divorce and then again after Robert's death, she and I had *dined* — that is precisely the right word, we dined — at a private table on the patio of the Gamelan, the toniest restaurant in downtown Asheville. And in my memory there is a thin wall between the two dining experiences, the two hellish rooms of memory.

I imagine an open door between the rooms.

Time passes, yet I return to that imaginary doorframe where I remember her words and my words. I hear there and I remember and actually recognize there the horrors inside the words we spoke. At the threshold of the recollection I find I can never tightly shut the door between the room of killing fire and the room of killing smoke.

"We finished him, didn't we?" she'd said. We had ordered our food. Our wine was very good, and the service was always excellent; the bread in little pieces. She had nodded, agreed: the bread pieces had been pinched but not sliced, that was a good touch. We liked being in a restaurant with good touches.

At both of our dinners at the Gamelan: wine good, service excellent, bread pinched, the main course fragrant, tasty farm-to-table fare before farm-to-table was all the rage. We ordered exactly the same food at both occasions when we'd dined together: the lawyer and the person called Samantha Peabody.

This account is inaccurate, naturally; however, Samantha Peabody's heart and mind have done their imagining and their calculus, so all of this, on the whole, is more essentially true than if each part were accurate.

"We did," Samantha Peabody said. "We finished him."

The process of meatifying a human occurs gradually. In order to effectively hound Robert, I divorced my self from my self. I needed Carla to assist Samantha Peabody in putting on the armor that felt good once all the various parts were fixed to me, a pitiless, relentless person.

Robert was weak and wounded and frozen in fear at the last stages of the divorce.

The absorbent bread sucked in the coppery green dipping oil. As if licking blood from each other's dripping jowls, our smiles were wet. Carla and I were proud of our flensing operations.

"The nephew and niece. Now that was a stroke of genius." The lawyer said she had always used her "bathosphere" technique, placing the divorcing man in an iron suit, sealing him off from any support, sending him down to the airless dark of his own guilt, controlling his light, his tether, his oxygen, his descent and his rate of ascent. But she had never thought to include children in the strategy until Samantha Peabody had told her about his love for his younger brother's two children, who were eleven and nine.

"He loves them," Samantha Peabody, already formulating the outcomes of subtractive force, had told her lawyer.

"They love him — kind of madly — the way children can do."

Samantha Peabody didn't have words for how Robert's love for the children, Thomas and Frida, was caught up in the bond between him and his brother. Robert and Tim had more or less parented each other after their own parents' divorce and visitation agreement. As adults they had felt awe about how Tim's firstborn, Thomas, made it uncannily possible for them to pull down walls of separation, to share themselves each to each with that child there between them at the crib, on the floor or, later, on the grass or, later yet, at the handlebars of the tricycle and the training-wheel bicycle. With Tim's second child, Frida, as with the first, the brothers could have the pure play of wild-growing, shadow-discovering fragile childhood; they could forget the old grieving.

Samantha Peabody found no difficulty in making Thomas and Frida hate their uncle. In her life as a scientist, she had studied sonic deformations in which one animal's call is interrupted by another that instantaneously changes both the message and the reception for all hearers. Unbounded human love converts more swiftly and totally to hatred in children than in love-stingy adults. Children's cruelty, Samantha Peabody understood, was so extraordinarily commonplace because their capacities for loving carried them to the outer limits of converging opposite emotions. In nature so many old eat their young. A great deal more often, the young eat the old.

This conversion of Thomas and Frida was done in a single weekend visit from their Aunt Sam. The children hated Robert: an oddly simply achievement.

They would not talk with him on the telephone. Time with him in person was out of the question. The children did not know how to explain why to him. They hated him so absolutely they did not wish for the opportunity to say to him, "Aunt Sam says . . ."

Aunt Sam had asked Frida and Thomas to tell her their feelings about how Uncle Robert "threw his family away"; how he had a brother, their dad, he'd thrown away, and a wife, their Aunt

Sam, he'd thrown away; how he had Thomas and Frida in his life and he threw them away like you throw away the napkins you use to blow your nose.

"Do you feel thrown away?" Aunt Sam asked Frida and Thomas. "If you feel thrown away, you can tell me, because I have been thrown away — or you can tell your dad. He got thrown away by Uncle Robert," Aunt Sam said. They did not, of course, need to tell her anything; the phrase "thrown away" would not travel out of them. Their hearing invited their hearts to fix the auditory clot in place so that everything they knew and felt about their Uncle Robert disappeared behind the expression, "thrown away."

Though Robert was a person of few words, he trusted the ponderable and imponderable effects of the human voice. In this case, he had no idea how to explain, how to ask them to understand. My assumption is that he thought it might be wrong to impose on them in that way. What would he say to Thomas and Frida? Would he ask, "Why do you hate me?" He understood they could not answer or, in any case, could not answer in a way that would help them — or him.

*

(Sometimes I can't orient myself in this album. I have moved down-creek in memory but I seem to be remembering a moment that occurred up-creek.

I pretended to feast on your two red baseball caps.

Your heads went in and the creek carried your caps away.

You said, "I could hear how cold it was." You said, "I liked it.")

*

I had surmised the children's father would collaborate with me, and I was correct. After all, at that particular moment in their lives, perhaps more than at any point in their distant childhood, Tim and Robert loved each other as if they were children. Like children they could be guided.

*

"Do you know," the lawyer said when she'd ordered her dessert, "do you know your husband phoned me asking me to help him understand how I could ever put you up to that trick with Frida and Thomas?"

He had phoned her. A lawyer more scrupulous than his lawyer would have advised strongly against calls at that particular time, but Robert often phoned Carla then and listened to her version of how he should act, what he should do.

I thought of his face, his pale-green eyes. I thought of his mouth, his vocal instrument perfect for whistling words. I asked him to learn birder's whistling-speech, and he taught himself — with manual in hand (F. Schuyler Mathews's *Field Book of Wild Birds and Their Music*) — to pronounce-express. At my worst times, if I asked, he would offer me his awfulest American robin; he would whistle-say, *Cheer-up! Cheeri-ly — cheeri-ly — cheer-up!* He would whistle-say a version of a scarlet tanager sounding like the musician Sting in The Police days: *Kwerit kwer kweree kwerit wer —*

My choice of dessert was the mousse. The lawyer's choice was also the mousse, which had a playful musical name of some kind. The lawyer plunged in her long pewter spoon, and opened her mouth wide and took in the taste. She gazed past the restaurant's glutton-herd and the servant-herd at Samantha Peabody. "Try this," she said. "It makes up for everything."

*

I put them on the trail ahead of me, and I saw her wave to us, and I did not wave back.

At our campsite we emptied the packs, took our new supplies down-creek to store the food. After we cabled up the canister, and listened to the satisfying ga-ulpt-ulpt-ulpt of the sleet striking the plastic skin, we set out for the pillow-and-cradle expedition.

I carried our camouflage, our eye protection, and our three weapons (and our three lesser weapons) in my frame pack.

The sleet had not relented, and the long veils of morning sunlight glinted as they danced away from us and farther away. As the woods now darkened, we could hear everywhere around us the general size of sounds inside the trommelling sleet.

We needed to make two creek crossings at fairly shallow places. We removed our shoes and socks there and rolled up our pants legs. It makes no sense to do that ever at a crossing. I commanded us. I could. I did. Nonsensical. And refreshing.

At the second crossing, the younger one did not re-clothe when we reached the other side. She looked at the icy rain striking her bare feet, she looked into the bleak woods, and she seemed physically quite uncomfortable, yet inside her hood, she giggled. A toad-trill giggle.

"I missed you, too," I said.

"Do you like her glasses?" asked the one.

The glasses had the same little sunflower decoration on each stem. They fit her nose, but the frames were too large for her face, which gave her the appearance of a failed experiment in exotic style.

✳

(I wonder about you. I summon your faces. Why would I ever wet paper with ink unless I wished for the stain to spread beyond its first aching?)

✳

"They're fake," said the one.

I said to the other, "*Dress*," and she toad-trilled as she put on her socks and shoes.

"They're fake," said the one, wishing to make sure both of us heard. "They don't correct anything at all. They just make her feel better."

The other gazed at me. She gazed at her older sister. The sleet pelted her hood, she drew her head further into it, and vapor came from her mouth.

She smiled at us with love. With love she met our curious gazes. She said, "They make me feel better. They really do." And she said, "Anyway. War says I need them."

"Warren?" I asked.

"He bought them for me."

"*Warren?*" I asked.

The two offered me nothing.

Near the creek was a tree, almost twelve meters in height, astride a large boulder. I asked them to sit at the base with me so we could listen for a moment to the tree transmitting the storm.

How did the tree sound?

I forget.

Their voices a semitone apart in pitch, the one and the other sang the name of the tree: "Yellow birch." Later that night I wrote a field note in order to remember the sound of their voices: *YEL-lowbirch — falling inflection — dominant, blue-violet or violet-blue in soundcolor.*

We faced the path ahead, watching the exchange of sleet and sunlight occur: the veils of sunlight moving forward in the dark silvered woods, the sleet sheathed in the sunlight.

Having waited out the storm, we walked again. I pointed out a coppiced shrub thicket; in late September, months earlier, I had heard a white-winged dove, completely hidden from view inside that thicket, asking a barrage of cooing questions: *"How-come-so-far?" "Hooker-are-you? Hoooooker?"* And, earnestly, sounding like Robert in his attempt to sound like Sting: *"Who-cooks-fer-ya?"*

Side note here: I may have been hearing a barred owl communicating with a white-winged dove. I continue my investigations.

We walked swiftly but with soft footfalls. I did not factor in their shorter strides; after all, the two were lighter and more agile than I. I was trying to move us along in order for us to explore the soundscape of that weird otherworld the locals called Hugo's Swipe. The Swipe was named for the storm of 1938 that brought a blowdown like none seen in these woods until the blowdowns occurring in the hurricane season of 1989.

They understood that we should not talk, but they could not help themselves. The other said her sock had gone down into her shoe. The one said, exactly as I would have, that it was not therefore the appropriate sock or shoe — or foot. The other said, "I need to fix it."

I guided us to a sitting place near a stand of mature beech and maple familiar to me because of Drummer bringing me there when I divorced Robert in October 1998, and bringing me there again when he died in late October 1999. Drummer and I had been friends then, and only friends.

*

On each occasion that Drummer brought me there, she had proposed that it would be good for us to kill something with her .22, a Remington 550 her grandmother had given her.

Under these same trees Drummer and I had sat perfectly still for six to eight hours at a time. We looked up into the leaf-glim now and then, but mostly we listened. With the reverence of killers, we listened.

Without speaking many instructions, Drummer showed me how to carve a figure from a piece of coal with our knives and our fingernails and teeth. She held up hers: the head of a black bear, eyes closed and mouth open. She gave me the what-is-it look when I held up mine.

Our hands were black. Our mouths and lips and teeth were black.

Twice she lifted her rifle at a tranquil, terrible moment, and said, "Catch!" which was of course impossible.

Both times I tried to catch the bloody squirrel-missile.

Our hunting expedition had been a good idea. The peaceful stalking and the calm killing and the not-catching gave me some temporary ease. Learning the methods of coal carving had also put me a little more at rest.

Once I had achieved an oval shape in the coal, I had tried to carve the form of a female white pine cone with my knife, nicking myself in the process. In order to define the seed scales, I used small bites and scrapes of my eyeteeth, and I suggested the wings and wing terminals with my fingernails. When I accidentally nicked myself, Drummer gestured for me to rub the blood into the carving. She asked if I agreed with her that blood was a beautiful color.

I said, "You high?"

"You're agreeing with me?"

"Not as a policy," I said. A person who lives alone will contemplate the question that she should suppress, the question that should instantly pass, the seriously weird question and the silly one. Inside the shadows of thought are the deepening shadows, and a person in great solitude invites the quickenings. I, for instance, have often contemplated a hardback copy of *The Voice That Is Great Within Us* (an anthology, published in 1970, Hayden Carruth as editor) set on a bar counter under five red bricks. Butterflies — swallowtails, sulphurs, and fritillaries — had been pressed inside the seven-hundred pages.

I can see the actual book: blacks, tigers, and giants, dog-faces, crescentspots and checkerspots flattened there through the decades, passed from one relict person to another in Stanley's~~Acker's~~Stanley's Bar in the town of Cord. Minister Stanley had opened the bar, then lost it to K. Acker; when he regained ownership from her, he crossed through Acker's name and insistently reasserted his own.

All these years later, alone in my tent, I experience the everyday anamnesis in which I wonder about the book under the bricks. No one could read the book, because too many gossamer lives were overwintering there. I find myself wishing to ask someone, *People brought in the butterflies, brought them with them to the bar? And they handed over the creatures in their flushed or faded cycle of color, caught on the drift or the stall, in the air or on the ground? And they placed each butterfly between two poem-faces, and pressed hard, and put the book back under the bricks, and asked for a drink?* I am aware that in a so-called "normal" conversation, I would ask about this at the most inappropriate time. And I would ask, Did the regulars just do that — regularly?

Apparently, they brought them in for Acker, then for Stanley, and for Acker again. I would ask about this at the Ambler's Market in Mill River while the cashier was talking with the bag boy, and I would ask at Ethel's Guns & Ammo, at Parlance Army Surplus. And I would ask, "Do you think Acker hated books that much?"

I'd asked Drummer, "Have you been to Acker's Bar in Cord?"

Drummer had said, "I think you mean Acker's~~Stanley's~~Acker's Bar. That book! Man, that's a lot of butterfly mash! You ever thought about collecting rabbit's blood? We could thin it and have us different tones of color we could work with."

"Drummer." I pushed her chin hairs down with my thumb. "What will become of you?"

She had so many things on her mind! "That's a bad way to go — mashed into a book."

"Drummer."

"What will become of me?" She had said, "You'll take care of me." She lifted her rifle, shot another. "Catch!"

*

The one asked me about the storm, "It stopped?" and for a moment I was fairly sure that she had read my mind. No, I wanted to say, it never stops but I can hide from it sometimes: how I learned what Robert had done, how all my misshaping and murdering of him began, how empowered I felt when making him utterly powerless, how I could not live with what I had done.

The trees shrugged off liquid crystals. The morning veils of light became lifting blades quietly withdrawing from their sheathings.

We were at the edge of the pillow-and-cradle field. Both of them stopped walking. Very softly, they stepped, they stepped. Looking at this place changed their center of gravity.

Within our sight now was The Black Tongue, a seventy-five-year-old fire-blasted oak snag. It was surrounded by the faint evidence of an octagonal mouth made of timbers four or five feet high. One would almost think an oddly constructed tourist-attraction fence had been built around the split snag.

When I explained more about the snag's strange housing, they were sure I was lying. They probably still disbelieve.

The hurricane of 1938 made plenty of news in the papers, but the resulting extremely violent blowdowns in this range were more or less ignored because of the number of other fantastic hurricane-devastation stories everyone told in the towns and cities. This occurred before my time, of course. But there was evidence. There was a large watercolor painted by Horace "Preacher" Ellington in 1940, framed nicely for everyone to see in Monteath's Asheville Auto Repair. The oldest Monteath, who is nearly deaf, becomes more deaf if you ask him about the hurricane. Drummer has told me that he is a distant relative of Preacher.

The watercolor has no lines, I recall. Preacher, spreading the wet pigment into the almost-dry pigment, must have felt that all definition had given way in that desolate place.

The blasts of wind had come from one source, and they blew down the trees all in the same direction. The trees, some of them over a hundred feet tall, were knocked down so hard the trunks folded the ground, the limbs pierced it, and the roots roared out, throwing tons of earth into the air. The expulsions created deep holes wreathed with root-whorl shapes. The hundreds of these wind-harrowed voids are as calming to the eye as all nests, and that's how people came to call them "cradles."

At first, we did not walk inside the pillow-and-cradle formation. We stepped up and stepped down into smaller and larger faults. I asked them to go in the direction of the oak snag and to call back when I called.

The one nudged her sister. She said, "I — I — my ears are ringing."

The other said, "Huh?"

"Lots."

"Mine too." The younger sister smiled horribly at me because a slight but tormenting straw of fear tickled her.

I brought out our SuperBlasters, water guns "Made for Serious Play," according to the manufacturers. I also assembled our net-guns, Weaver Class M Series Web Launchers, in the methodical manner I had practiced since seeing the two for the March Sonic Adventure. Drummer and Park Ranger Ruck — her real name: Ellenby Ruck — had helped me in my efforts to acquire this equipment.

"This is the wrong place to be," I said. "Do you feel that?"

She did. They both did. Good teacher that I am, I allowed a pressured silence that caused them to walk farther, to leave me. I once again adjusted my daypack holding the sealed fruit juice containers that we would eventually empty into the SuperBlasters.

They took almost fifteen minutes to get to the snag one hundred fifty feet away. They had no choice but to walk into the deep holes and, in most cases, climb onto the odd pillows made by seven decades of the root-fists releasing dirt into the cradles. Then they had to climb out.

At the snag, the one called, "Pea!" but remembered she was supposed to wait until I called. She did not call out again.

I could not see either of them.

*

(I lost you. You wished to be lost. I wished that for you.)

*

I allowed a distance and silence in which the three of us could hear the soft tongue-blade of bee sounds and far-out-of-view vulture calls reverberate against these cavities and convexities.

There was a food cable in the woods nearby, a taut cable that the sleet played like a pennywhistle.

I called out, "Are you safe?"

"Probably." That is what I heard. Or, I heard, "What, Pea?" Or — "Possibly." I assumed the answer was "Possibly," since that was the kind of mocking of Samantha Peabody the one and the other offered on such occasions.

"Touch the snag," I said. I left behind the assembled guns and the unchambered missiles; I left the SuperBlasters. I covered them carefully with muslin Drummer had given me.

I walked down. Inside the large crater containing so many smaller craters, I moved toward them.

"Touch it," I said.

"Huh?" said the other.

"Touch The Black Tongue."

No answer.

I thought I heard a tock-tick-tocking absorbed and resorbed by the pillows and cradles. I thought I heard my heart's gears straining, and I felt the percussions of my lungs. When I reached the two they were running counterclockwise circles, and they each had sticks they clicked against the ruined boards surrounding the snag.

"You don't want to?" I said. I could see that they were about to resume their noisy game. I said, "I want to touch it — I want it to touch me."

"Don't," said the other.

"Pea —" said her sister.

"Excuse me." My hands lingered there.

"Ewww," said the other. The lenses of her useless glasses shone. She was alert. Her ardent, constant mind concentrated on the acts of creation occurring before her.

"I see a microscope in your future," I said to her.

I walked into a gap in the fence-like octagon. I did not expect a response since the child knew me, knew I would not say more.

I touched the inside grooves of the forked tongue. I wrapped my arms around the stiff muscle of it. I listened.

I heard the sound of tapping against the smooth skin of an American beech. The sound belonged in this phytosonic field, but only barely belonged, and the tapping repetitions were in a pattern.

I felt pleased to know of those presences in the woods. Drummer. Ruck.

I put my face against the snag. I breathed through my nose, closed my mouth. I signaled the two children to be absolutely still.

And I could hear more. And they could hear with me.

For years I had heard the three human voices in the woods during certain days and nights in the pillow-and-cradle field. They called each other by their first names, Ricky, Chad, and Case; through the years, Drummer and I had been able to help the U.S. Park Police and the law enforcement division of Wildlife Resources identify them.

In April every year at the same time the three began setting out their bait in order to poach feral swine and black bear. The pillow-and-cradle field and the surrounding woods had been their most successful sites.

Case had a weathered, emphysemic voice. Chad and Ricky, his sons and abetters, sounded metagnathous; when Ruck showed Drummer and me their file photos — cited and fined over the years, they and their father had always dodged the thirty days they should have served in jail — it was apparent that the boys' jaws had been broken in the past. For a very short period of time, they would have been handsome boys. They might have recognized their gentler natures in their own features. Case, his own jaw broken more than once, had corrected that for them.

They perennially returned to the scene of their crime because they were stupid. Or because the fines were small, and the years of cutbacks in the Park Police force made arrest more and more unlikely.

On one of their night hunts in late May, 2000, Drummer had called them by name in the woods. "Here, Ricky! Here, Chad!" And like the true haint she was, she'd shrieked: "Case! Case! Heeeeeere, Case!"

Their dog Gooser had howled and circled his own tail. The three froze in place.

Walking up to them out of the dark, I took one very good deer-in-the-headlights picture of Case. He had an abnormally large skull, the battering-ram skull of an old flathead catfish.

And while they were still recovering from the camera flash, I stepped back into the darkness, and said, "I hunt here, too."

As they retreated, Drummer and I taunted them from our separate places in the dark. "Chad! Ricky! Case!" Fortunately, Gooser was confused by Case pissing himself. Gooser lay down near the snag and would not leave with his masters.

He is Ruck's dog now, and Drummer tells me that when she wants a laugh, she will say, "Do Case, Gooser," and Gooser will make a mewling rubato *ggawph-ggawph-gggggawwwph-aaawwwwwph-aaaaaawp* bark-cough. Operatic. Emotional.

Of her inappropriate collusion with Drummer and me, Ranger Ruck had said, "That's bad form." Of Drummer and me in our continuing battle with the three poachers, she'd said, "That's really bad form."

When I brought the one and the other to the gun cache, they were very definitely disapproving, though they were only mildly surprised. Their mother had forbidden them to use point-and-shoot video games or toy guns of any kind and, they explained, she "freaked" if they played with children who played with any form of weapon.

The netguns caught their attention rather immediately. I showed them that they were like shotguns but not as heavy as they looked. I explained the use of the ground tripods, the loading of the cartridges containing the compressed nets. The two looked at me with no comprehension. Explaining was never my strong point. I could present a specimen and contextualize observations, and I could introduce a concept and frame premises, but confoundment was my specialty.

"They're — they're — what *are* they for?" the one asked.

"They are problem solvers," I said.

The other tugged at me. "Betty means —"

I said, "They are missile launchers. Beautiful ammunition, is it not?" I lifted up one of the cartridges. They were not reloadable. We would need twenty-seven net missiles for practice, nine for execution.

The one asked, "And —?"

"These are SuperBlasters, they are quite effective mega-juicers," I said, "and the hunt will end with them."

We practiced briefly with the SuperBlasters, which were light and easy to manage even when fully loaded with liquid.

With and without the tripods, we practiced shooting our net-guns for three hours that day because, after all, that same night would be our hunting night.

During our lunch, I explained that we were going to "collect" Case, Chad, and Ricky for arrest by the appropriate agencies. I wanted the two to understand that we were going to do this without causing the men more than discomfort.

The one swallowed down water, took another nibble at her turkey jerky. "Does our mom know about this?"

I said, "I wanted to tell her. She was not prepared for that information."

"Unprepared," said the one.

The other nodded, looking down at her creeping socks. She asked, "Is this a bad idea?"

Generally — yes: that is what I meant to say at the time, though I did not. I am acknowledging now my bad idea to alter the ecosystem by removing such parasites as the three poachers. And there is no justification — simply none — for a person with scientific training and the company of two intelligent, adventurous children to use weapons in this way.

At the time, I said, "Have you looked closely at the structure around The Black Tongue?"

Their silence answered: yes, they had looked closely.

My silence invited them to listen to my breathing in order to read my mind. This was possible if I made it possible.

The one asked, "That place — something about that place is — is — isn't right."

Inside the so-called fence they had heard: underneath their feet was not simply earth but earth held in a wooden vessel almost fourteen meters deep, its circumference 3.6576 meters at the narrowest point. What looked like a fence was, in fact, the strange giant cup's pine-board lip. I did my best to help them understand that the two of them could be echolocaters, that seeing-inside is impossible but hearing-inside is not. The eye is not capable of doing more than locating a hollow place in the earth; the eye can see the mouth of a cave but cannot see farther than light can reach. The ear and the hearing chambers of the body and the throat and head and sinuses and the skull's empty crevices find the deepest chambers of the cave and, with relative accuracy, they formulate the depth and scale of those chambers. When one reaches into the earth in this hearing-inside way there is no longer two but one: the earth-you calls back.

"There is a giant earth-cup below you," I said. I asked, "Have you heard?"

"An earth-cup," said the other. She found the idea appealing. Her sister sneered at her.

The storm of 1938 had lifted the steeple off the St. Blaise Church. Wind had flown it almost half a mile across the sky. The sturdy structure speared into this place in the woods. On the way it had whistled — Old Woman Tozan over in Birtleville told me this — *"eee-ou-EEE-ou-ee-ou-EEE-ou."* Pure vowels. I love a pure vowel. I prefer a pure vowel over a click. Back when I had regular contact with humans and I would hear a human vocalization with more tappings than tones, all I heard was frenetic clatter, noise but not sound, signaling but not singing.

The missile-steeple had arrowed in at almost no angle.

Wind and tides of micro-quakes rocked the timbered larynx. Over the decades the open chamber tilted and arighted, filled with leaves, with sloughed-off bark, with twigs, with branches of great size, with creatures who wandered in and could not work their way out, with rainwater, with plants that took root but withered and were baked by the trapped heat.

I would like to be buried in this womb filled with decay, brimmed with earth and life.

*

(You may visit me there.)

*

We left our guns under their muslin cloth cover near the earth-cup. We retreated to the yellow birch under which the younger child had stalled out earlier in the day. It was dusk now and.

I helped them put on their camouflage, very light space-age material, fitting the Velcro at their throats and wrists and ankles, pulling the cord on their hoods, two-seamed hoods that made little bubbles over their ears, and.

I smoothed the material over their heads; I smoothed their ears and.

I like to remember. The little vulnerable heads in my untrustworthy hands. I regret almost everything between humans and me, blame myself for being a waste of bone structure, of watery flesh, skin, and.

I smoothed their socks up their ankles. Green socks, I laced their boots more tightly to make them safe though uncomfortable, I chalked their noses and cheeks with school chalk, I subdued their grins with chalk drawn around their mouths, I touched my hushing-finger over their lips, and.

The remembering is so good that I always want to write and and and, and this album gets bigger than I had planned.

*

(Do you remember? I wonder: remember that you Velcroed me, smoothed me, sock-checked and chalked me?)

*

We invited the tree to transmit what it heard. We listened to the crepuscular soundscape, the explorations of creatures neither nocturnal nor diurnal, neither singing nor saying. In their twilight-humming, time-passing surged in them, stopped full and started and stopped full.

The creatures were not silent, alone.

They were not silent. Silence is an unsearching aura and causes aloneness.

They were quiet. Quiet searches to the futural edge of the void and the vista, meets quiet with quiet: a sonic halo like the halo the sky's last rays of light make in the holy hours.

We heard a slapping sound. In the woods, not so far from us, bare fingertips were lightly tapping resonant tree trunks.

"Who is it?" asked the one.

The tapping seemed to answer her.

The other said, "Oh."

I gave them the gifts of carved bear and pine cone. The bear, small enough to fit entirely in the one's hand, had been patiently finished. I would guess that Drummer had used the wood paste she used on all of her woodcarvings. The mixture of olive oil and beeswax was often on her fingers, and I liked the taste. The tiny bear, a perfect totem of ferocious mute fullness, had a pleasant smell, as if Drummer had crushed mint leaf and rubbed every part with that concoction.

The other held the pine cone I had carved. She moved it in her hands. She wanted to ask, What? She wanted to ask, How?

I have made so many coal carvings since then. I have specialized in the ovuliferous female cones on which the prickle has formed. I am glad she has — if she has it still — my first effort, which was not made to scale and which looked something like a child's mummified finger.

I had given the older child a flawless hand-sewn cloth bag in which to place the bear; and for the younger child's pine cone I provided a plastic harmonica case (the sliding-open Lee Oskar kind).

"Let us hunt," I said.

We huddled.

"You know what to do?" I asked.

"Got it," said the other.

"Got it," said the one.

I said, "You must shoot slowly, deliberately. Remember that, you two."

I said, "Let's not die today."

April 30 – May 6, 2004

My tent was my tower, garret, crystal palace, croziered chamber, gauntlet, bucket seat, crawlspace, my secret garden. I took a long bending draw from my C harp, making my wish: to glow inside the glowing sound. One can accurately apply the chemical term for the fixed stability of that sound: luciferin.

I said, "I have six more."

"Yes," said the other sleepily acceding. It was almost midnight, the first night of the May sonic adventure.

"Mmmhmm," said the one in a knowing voice on the fringe of audibility. She knew — I'm guessing she knew that I was counting the six more months I would have with them. I was not counting down to my withdrawal from the rest of the world.

They heard.

I believe they heard.

I sang, "*I went down to St. James Infirmary. / I saw my baby there. / She was stretched out —*"

In the woods wind was fighting ground. From the creek came

the scent-sounds of mild breeze breathing upon staminate and pistillate flowers. Straggler hog sphinx moths whipped their quirt bodies against the tent skin. Just before dark there had been a dive-bombing phalanx of them, and I had to explain to the one and the other that the threatening two-inch-long creatures were in a dreaming state that included us only because we had camped in their pleasuring zone.

Other goblin sounds came from the woods. *Elaphe obsoleta obsoleta* the black rat snake was eating starling fledglings stashed half-alive in some shallow depression near us.

I was pleased to be able to play the notes of "St. James Infirmary" somewhere deep inside me where the song isn't at all owned by exactitude. Huge had taught me to play the exact melody late in the song, in the second-to-the-last or the last bar, a way to have the harp sing, *This is where I might have been if I had stayed.*

I held the two close against me, the one on my right and the other on my left. The other's left hand was over my heart, sometimes palm-clapping me very slightly. The one pressed the top of her head under my right ribcage. Her head rocked upward, burrowed into me.

They were drifting off.

At times like this time, I would make confessions I shouldn't, certain that what they heard while they were more or less asleep would dissolve.

From my side embouchure I pulled another bending draw into my chest and bronchially rattled the note. *Now when I die I want you to bury me in my silk suit and my best top hat.* / *A*

*twenty-dollar gold piece hanging off my watchfob. / I want the
boys to know I died standing pat.*

I told them everyone more or less understood that the song
was about a man visiting his lover, dead of venereal disease. The
man is dying of the same. Huge had told me no one knows who
wrote the song. He said, "I never do want to know who wrote
something or painted a picture or what." He could see I wasn't
agreeing, and he said, "To care about who made a song — about
who made the song first — that's the original sin of everybody
who thinks they're so damn original."

"Venereal disease is — well, unpleasant," I said now to the two
deep-asleep snorers.

"And I miss Huge like I cannot begin to say. I will — this is in no
way an exaggeration — I feel like I will never get over him —"

The last of the moths struck the tent with small punches of
unworded music. I listened to the tree bark flaking off in the
woods, and thought I heard perfect pronunciations of *"chop —
check-check — chip — check."* Trees undressing have something
to disclose.

"I would give anything to have one more lesson with Huge."

I played in order to bring his ghost. I practiced shifting from one
side embouchure to the other, and I was slobbery because I was
not controlling my breath at the front of my mouth. But also
because there was my nose leaking tears.

There were my hands trembling. There were my throat's
bad-plumbing sounds. I tried to explain that he taught me
blues music, after all: a way to sing the murderous, celebratory

joys inside the most killing griefs.

I said that I was full of shit, too. I just plain missed Huge. Years ago, at the first lesson, he asked me why I wanted to learn harmonica. "I want to have a soul I can put my mouth to," I would have said if I could have thought of something so shapely. I asked, "Do I have to know?" and he did not give an answer.

I went on and on about what I said and he said, about what might have been said, what should have been said. One would think I was Elaine.

At daybreak, I was actually hoarse from talking and singing and playing. And the tip of my tongue was sore, and my mouth hurt because of all the rough kissing and tongue-blocking and tongue-tapping upon the harp. I left in order to visit the empire of the worms. For a long time, my companion among them, Old Peeko, has been fed by and has fed himself to the dark under-earth. More than once through the years I have stretched him to his full length, have subdivided him with the fingernails of my thumb and first finger.

And to this very day we are friends. May is his mating season. He is not opposed to many young Peekos reproducing.

At sunrise when I entered the tent with my feet and legs shining, the two were not gurgling my name, but they were stirring.

So I fitted myself between them in order to fore-hear. And, then, to hear: "Pea — Pea — Pea." The other more or less echoed the one.

The plan for the day — every expedition day of the sonic adventures was well planned — had been reviewed the night before: we would prowl the area near our food site, agreeing to spend the morning on all fours and to stand only after our lunch. This was the perfect day for our prowling because the clouds had settled on the mountains and were settling further down instead of lifting. If our bodies were low enough to the ground we would hear sounds radiating down through the other sounds and we would hear the sounds held beneath, and we would have to hear as ground creatures hear. That was the lesson plan.

I asked them to clean their glasses and leave them in their cases.

The other left hers on. She used the toggle to tighten her eyeglass cord.

On all fours, we crawled out of our tent.

I had poured enough water for the three of us into a single bowl set on a cooling stone, but I had not expected that we would all drink at the same time and in such a spirit of accommodation, and with such concentration that our chins were wetted as we cat-lapped at the bowl. And I had not expected we would leave our faces unwiped.

How do I remember such moments? I wonder.

❋

(And I wonder: How would I ever forget?)

❋

Against my advice, they wore their green mittens, which made each movement more tiring by effectively cancelling out the spring of their fingers as they advanced on their hands and knees.

The other had a natural long and loping stride. Her shoulders rolled, her head rocked up and moved slightly side to side. The one covered more space before each stop, but hers was a pounce-drag-pounce pattern that caused her to raise her head and huff a little and lower it again. Needless to say, they paid no attention to the excellent example of Samantha Peabody who, despite her sixty-seven-year-old frame, moved effortlessly on her knees and her bare front paws and rear paws. Samantha Peabody's aligned but relaxed head and body and hips glided her forward and stopped her without so much as the snap of a twig or crunch of a seedpod.

We stopped often. We stopped at full alert, our butts up. We stopped on our back haunches. We stopped fully prone. Through the receptive chambers of our chests and throats and bellies and hipbones we heard things we could not hear were we upright.

Only a dozen yards from our campsite, a raptorial sound clawed over our backs and compressed our bellies. We shivered when the same signal repeated. How does sound that terrible gorge on you and make you feel repletion in the same instant?

A brutally short shriek came next, then a sound the same length as the first sounds to which we had reacted.

I whispered, "Have you heard?" They rubbed their sides against my sides. The one draped her head and neck over my neck; the other gripped her head over my shoulders, her jaw digging in.

"What?" said the other in a kind of biting down.

I said, "Wait."

They were trembling.

I said, "Wait. Wait."

A grinding scream over one hundred fifty years old. A hungering, hunting squeal that rumbled into the woods from beyond the world and all its words.

The furnace of sound had a maw that seethed, and a sinuous rattling tail. It made the sound of strained haspings, of bass drumming moving away, of subterranean growling.

It began to leave us.

The continued existence of the sounds endured in the same way that speeding cars' taillights streak the air behind them.

"We will rest here," I said when the full terror let us go.

They still jawed me, necked me, as if from within.

"Okay, Pea," said the one, asking, "tell us."

"It has horns," I said.

Some silences are more naked than others.

I said, "It can never go any way but the way it has always gone." I made myself supine.

Supine, I did some settling- and some squirming-in, and a good pine-needle scent came up from the ground under the muscles of my bottom.

"Try it," I said, and they did: they pushed their spines and hips down, the backs of their heads, they purr-laughed, almost instantaneously able to shiver off and splash themselves clean of fear, and when I lifted my arms and legs into the air they did the same, they bug-wiggled the same as I, their shoes and mittened hands twitching in the air.

In the unique conditions of the atmosphere that day, the screams had come for us from at least forty terrain-amplifying miles west. They had warned us with two longs, a short, and a long.

We pretended we could not get aright.

I said, "We have to put ourselves back on our paws."

We converted, and after a few feline push-ups, some arching of our backs, some self-satisfying neck stretching, we prowled up the path.

"The Norfolk Southern Railroad," I said, "that was the sound. The train on the tracks."

I asked, "And did you wish to know what became of the three men you netted?"

*

(You have learned by now that there are unexpected consequences to netting a person — or two, or three. Not all the consequences are negative. Ask Drummer.)

*

Drummer and Ranger Ruck, understanding the full set of consequences, threaded static rope through the net holding Case, and they hauled him to four feet from the ground, so that the two children could juice him thoroughly while he snarled and screamed.

"Little bitches! Little bitches!" screamed the dripping man in the storybook situation. To be a trapper who has been trapped by small children in fixed positions, calmly, accurately firing capture nets: that surely must have been Case's worst nightmare.

I accompanied the one and the other back to our camp, and only learned a week later that Drummer and Ranger Ruck had hauled Case as high as possible up the bear cable where, for many hours, he had swung wildly in his efforts to elude the biting ants, and to escape the flesh-eating sameness and the gut-gnawing otherness of every word he shouted out.

In the hours before he was let go, Case had opportunity to observe that when his sons Ricky and Chad were freed from their nets they neither came to his aid nor returned for him at a later time.

Drummer later accompanied Ricky and Chad to her home where she shared stew and fresh bread and weed with them. For a night, she gave them a safe place to stay, and she gave them moonshine that damaged them more wonderfully than other moonshine they had drank in the past. The next morning she sent the two hung-over runaways out of the woods with essential supplies that she placed in two large pickle-green canvas bags.

Not at all self-conscious about the goliath purses, they set off. They had a head start; but they must have felt they did not matter enough to Case that he would hunt for them once he was freed by Ranger Ruck and Drummer. Case must have known that Drummer would kill him and would cure his carcass on her front porch if he harmed Ricky and Chad.

*

In a pattern of succor that has continued to the present, Drummer has been an animal guardian to Ricky and Chad.

Ricky is a third-grade teacher. Chad has become a pharmacy assistant. They share a room in the Princess Artine Hotel in downtown Asheville.

Drummer has two human cubs. She netted them. They are hers. She is theirs. She tells me they are attentive to her. Ricky and Chad understand that they should keep their distance from me, but every Thanksgiving they come into my camp in the hours before I am awake. Drummer has given them the locations of my seasonal camps.

I hear them, they sound like Tom-ghosts clambering down and back up a magic vine. They leave me a cold turkey, about a fifteen-pounder, that they have carved perfectly. They leave me apple juice as a joking test of my memory, and they leave me green-apple pies, and how do they know I like fruit pie to be tart? They have packaged everything up in wax-paper-lined shoeboxes.

Not wishing to draw animals to my campsite, they say, "See ya, Sam," and they stand eight to ten feet from my tent, and they do not leave until they know I have heard.

I do not say back, "See ya," since that is simply not like Samantha Peabody. I take a little sipping draw from my Educator Chromatic harp, and that is their signal to leave. They do not matter at all to this album that is my poorly tilled patch. Yet they are leaves I cannot seem to rake away.

✻

"What about that old man?" asked the other about poor Case.

A burring note, the whistle-humming sound I like best in birdsong, came from a low limb near us. We were on our sides in a circle, our twelve paws pointing in, and I remembered F. Schuyler Matthews accounting for such song occurring under the "stress of gladness." I remembered that.

And in an instant I forgot for a very long time. And now, under the identical stress, I have remembered again.

✻

Hours after our trapping adventure, Ranger Ruck came to me and my two fellow trappers who had not, after all, died, though they felt the persistent mild sickness of remorse. She asked to take up the problem of freeing Case Curran. She explained that she lowered him almost to the ground but pulled him back up on the cable each time he threatened her. She lowered him completely to the ground that morning, and soaked him with buckets of creek water each time he lunged at her from inside the sticky web. She instructed him about the steps that he must take when she freed him: to undress completely, to be escorted on foot by her in order to turn himself in, to pay his fine, to never poach again. At any part of the instruction to which he reacted badly, she pulled him up a foot from the ground, spun him, soaked him with more cold water.

"I was not cruel," she said, "cruelty is not good policy for a Park Ranger."

"And?" I asked.

"I was firm," she said, "*firmness* I do believe in."

And when he was free of the net, completely naked and walking just in front of her per her orders, if Case was in any way threatening, Ranger Ruck allowed Gooser to bite at the shivering monster's ankles and calves and buttocks. Twice, Gooser did this so enthusiastically that a third time was not necessary.

I said I was thankful the two had not been there for that part. They heard but did not see Case's suffering.

"I'm sorry you had to hear," said Ranger Ruck.

"We like to hear," said the other. "We do," said the one, "but — but we — but you — what we did we shouldn't've."

*

On our way back from our adventure, we loped on all fours. We rubbed our flanks and necks and foreheads, our faces, our haunches and asses, against a black walnut tree that was a favorite of mine. We heard starling nestlings. The few fledglings there sounded terrified, as if the three prowling humans at the base of the tree really were felines. We did not intentionally purr in hungering response; our purring, a bird-tasting purring, simply occurred. I noted in my field journal that this had never occurred with other sonic adventurers. With these two, I noted the trans-individual voicing. I voiced what I felt in them and in the walnut, and they voiced what they felt in the walnut and in themselves and in the nestlings and fledglings, which caused me to voice what they voiced, all the voices in chorus, which caused the two, sounding more or less as one, to voice my voice.

I suppose this all happened only because of that day of rare climate, in the after-mast season, the rare physical state of the participants in the peculiar sonic liturgy. I suppose that explains, as well, what happened next.

After eating turkey jerky at our meal site, we removed our green woolen caps in order to wash our faces. It had been eight months since I first lowered their heads into the creek for them, and now they placed their faces in and, instinctively, their whole heads up to their necks.

I counted the seconds they were underwater.

They seemed to turn their faces toward each other there. I could discern what they were doing: they were listening. Their shoulders bunched upward. Their mittened hands tightened their grip on the bank.

Both heads exploded out of the water. "You win!" said the older one, exhilarated. The younger said, "I won! I win! I win!"

I had nothing to dry their heads with, so I showed them how to finger-comb and wring out each other's hair. They had never been shown how to do this. I made them shake out as much of the moisture as possible, and I fixed their green woolen caps over them.

The May air was cold at 2 PM when we entered the tent, and they were grateful to dry out better, to be turbaned up, to nap. Inside their sleeping bags they made a peeping sound; I clucked at them in the way a hen turkey would respond to her poults.

In May these woods are just right for the fairytale forms of napping. Through the years I have assiduously recorded this phenomenon. The woods cast the uprooting spell in April and March, the wilding spell in June and in February, the secret-spilling spell in July and in December, the riddling and riddle-compounding spell in August and in January. The woods cast the sleep-plunging spell in May and October.

I took one of their favorite books out of their hiding place. "Rather obvious stash site," I said, pulling out the volume.

"Rather," said the one who did not like me much at that moment.

"Rather," said the other.

A picture has formed in my mind: later in her life the other will have terrible figurative Samantha Peabody shingles-type pain arising from secret keeping. Many kinds of Samantha virus will have remained in her. Waiting.

I said, "*You are sleepy and weak. You are sleepy and weak weak and sleepy you are are are are you are weekeepy sleeky you are sleeweekeepeekey-yeekeepeepleekee-keeeepy. You are are . . . are . . . weesleeweesleepeekeepeesleeeeee.*"

They were not quite completely spell-struck. I read their favorite, *The Ice Cream Life of Lindsey & Lawrence Robertsondaughter-Fitzenghetollinghfuhl*, a book of approximately twelve thousand words. The author, Valentine Melusina, published this apocalyptic work in 1984; at the front of her book was the dedication, "For The Children of Wall Street." Homeless and alone, Melusina disappeared the very next year, assumed dead, a profitable convenience for Privilege

Publishers who have, so the 2002 cover says, "preserved this Beloved American Classic reprinted in 29 languages."

As they fell hard asleep I read them the final line: *Ice cream tastes best when none is left to share.*

I closed the book, and I returned it to the sleeve of the other's rain jacket. The left sleeve had two other books inside; the right sleeve had three books inside. No doubt, between them the one and the other had a total of at least ten books hidden up their raincoat sleeves.

The other woke up first. We gazed at each other; we smiled, remembering how we were when we were prowling the woods. She looked away, and I asked, "Something on your mind?"

Four days later at the trailhead parking lot, I understood.

*

Carl used her lawyer-graymother voice: "Get into the car with us, Samantha."

I sat between the two in the backseat. I did not put my arms around them. They pressed themselves against the doors.

Looking at us in the mirror, Carla said, "You — I have no choice but to say this within their hearing — you are aware my children are eight and six years old?"

"They are —"

"Be quiet. You are aware of my children's ages, two children who until now have had no awareness of *effing and mating.*"

They are quite aware, I wished to say. "I have made them aware of _distinctions_ between the two behaviors," I said, and did not say, _And you and your fuck-buddy the judge have assisted me in this important instruction._

Needless to say, I would have preferred that I could escape her rage.

And why had I not feared the rage of other Sonic Adventure parents for the repeated crime of cursing aloud, which was not a small crime even if I committed it only rarely? Because very young children, particularly the intelligent female children of graymothers, do not usually feel compelled to disclose their word-awakening experiences; by nature, they usually welcome more awakening instead of closing the door by telling.

Selfishly, utterly selfishly, I was not happy that the other had unburdened herself of that highly questionable part of my program of instruction.

I am sure I did not care about how it might have been difficult for this particular child to keep it all secret. I did not care.

And for what reason now, all these years later, would I ever forgive myself?

"I told her not to snitch," said the one.

"She didn't say bad words too much," said the other. To be certain her mother and sister heard her, she said, "Not much. Really."

And that was true: I chose only the appropriate seasons.

"Be quiet," said Carla. She very precisely recounted how the judge — the single greatest danger to her and to the well-being of her family of three — questioned her "maternal judgment and fitness." The letter was printed on his Office of Chief District Court Judge Warren Graham stationery, a letter to which was appended his full written report of the account the other had offered about the inappropriate and, according to him, obscene discourse of Professor Samantha Peabody: the same Professor Samantha Peabody in unsupervised contact with the above-mentioned children for fifty-six of the past two hundred forty days.

"You would consider this account as fact?" Carla asked.

"I would," I answered.

The one said, "I told her not to . . ."

The other.

Oh. The other.

I will stop now in order to sit with my Modern US Zone chromatic harmonica, a fairly junky vintage instrument that I play sometimes. When an amateur harmonica player wishes for the "jug-o-rum-more-rum" pond sound of giant bullfrogs, this is the instrument of choice. Devoted to diatonic harmonica, I am uniquely incompetent in playing my chromatic harmonica. I feel ashamed of myself when I play it.

※

All along, the other faced the car window. Her eyes were closed. She was not listening to any voice, sound, or noise inside the car. But she was, without a doubt, listening.

"Get out," said Carla to the three of us.

A blissed-out fetally coiled porcupine, a teenager, had eaten so much he was bloated and immobilized at the edge of the tiny pond. We put our ears to the creature's snout and heard: an ocarina recital. We listened. Our listening was or-listening; that is, we did not leave right away out of scorn or from respect for him, or from self-respect, or out of or inside the fear that he would awaken or we would awaken, or out of a sense there must be something better near us or on his path or on our own.

We sat next to him for as long as a full-length movie. The shallow pond, no more than twenty feet across, was in perfect recipience. Every puncturing sailmaker pine needle and dry thread of leaf spine plinked as it pierced the sensitive glass.

The porcupine woke up, rocked onto his back, and scratched at the whorled hair on his belly. Flexed his quills, relaxed them. Eyes squinting, he seemed to ask indignantly, *"Did you kiss me?"*

The one nodded no.

The other nodded no.

I looked askance because in the middle pages of my heart I felt he was a porcupine prince, and I had imagined giving him an innocent peck.

"Huh?" he said. *"Huh?"* His claws slowly curled and uncurled as if seeking two phantom tokes. His black-jellybean eyes gazed at the other, his smile bristling because of his adolescent spotty beard.

She gave him back as good as she got. "Huh?" she said to him.

"Huh-ah-ah. Huh-oo-uh." In a high key, he made the ocarina sound. He was going to return to his nap if we would only leave.

"She's not going to kiss you," said the one.

"True," said the other. She bowed and pored over him. Every part of her pondered him.

By now, she was contemplating kissing him.

I was contemplating the kiss.

The one was contemplating it.

Everyone knows that all drowning creatures were kissed as they entered the ark and kissed as they left. Lark, leopard, salamander, butterfly, wasp, hare, octopus, giraffe, beetle, hummingbird, turtle, viper, wolf, all wear the imprint of a kiss or the faint prehensile mark.

"Hoo-uh-ah. Hoo-hu-ah. Huh-oo. She was me once." He asked me, "Does she know?"

I was fairly certain he meant, *Does she know that she was a porcupine once?* He could have meant, *Does she know how good it is to be a porcupine?* He could have meant anything.

He flipped onto all fours. He gave us the make-way look.

He wanted to say something kind in order to acknowledge that we large creatures could have feasted on him and had not.

He walked away. Walked on. Stopped.

He muttered, *"I be QweT-Tek-KET Kwook-kkkwoTTee." Remember me."*

I have only slightly altered this account of QweT-Tek-KET the porcupine. I would be surprised to hear that my companions remember him differently.

✳

We were at a halfway point between our camp and Drummer's. In those days I had one permanent camp; now I have two other seasonal camps. I am impossible to find.

First daylight slowly opened the mouth of a deep, two-chamber surface cave near us, its overhanging ledge weeping water from a spring somewhere above. I explained that the one should not pitch her tent too near the pond. I had trained her well enough that she understood how many creatures come at night to a pond, how many surge and resurge from a pond's stratiform membranes.

I told her that Someone had long ago named this primitive camp Pilate's Washbowl because a blood-red dish-stone had been found there and taken away for some church Somewhere.

An adventure depends on someone like me who was The Someone to make up a convincing-sounding, threatening name for an unnamed place, and to reference a Somewhere the child adventurer would soon enough encounter.

This was the Blind Date part of the June sonic adventure, which was strictly for adventurers eight years old or older; I did not enter into a contract with grayparents who would not agree to this. In May I always confidentially checked with the child to be sure she felt comfortable with the Blind Date; if not, I allowed the child to opt out.

The one did not opt out. I had provided her with an ultra-light bivy tent, enough bedding, a water filter device, and a mini-flashlight. I had provided her with two maps that gave trail information about how to go from here to Drummer's and from Drummer's back to our camp.

The other and I set up the one in this campsite. I explained that her younger sister and I were returning to home camp. I emphasized that she would be alone, completely alone. Her three-day assignment: to stay in this primitive camp that night; to hike half an hour to visit Drummer in Mansour Cove the next evening and stay with Drummer; on the third day she would return alone to the home campsite where we would be waiting.

She had never met Drummer. I assured her, "She will be much like the witches in your storybooks, but with more teeth. She is affectionate and musty. She makes mumbling sounds out of her nose and mouth, and only some of them are words. She has Acrocanthosauran blistery lips. Her eyes have accumulated darkness for one hundred fifty million years."

"I don't —"

"You do not know her," I said. "She has seen the picture of you I took when you registered for the Sonic Adventure. She is expecting you."

They held hands. I said, "You should find where and how to isolate your food. You should examine the sonic contours around you by — how?"

"By listening," the other said, answering for her sister.

"You should not miss your nap. At night leave your tent only to urinate and defecate. Or bring your light outside with you and dance and sing. Or climb the bur pine, see it there, about twenty feet high? — check it first for creatures — and quietly climb out on one of the limbs and put your ear to one of the cones and —"

"She's kind of heavy," said the other.

"She is far too light to have trouble on a tree limb. Besides, even a four-hundred-pound bear couldn't crack the lowest limbs of a bur pine," I said. "Though — please note that I am not making this up — you should remember that a four-hundred-pound bear could climb up to meet you at any place in a bur pine."

I kicked the toes of her hiking boots. She kicked mine back.

"You will have to let go," I said to the two, who were still holding hands.

"Oh," they said more or less at the same time. And did not let go.

Then they let go.

"And one more reminder: day or night, the cave is good for exploring, a marvelous place with a rare fadeless soundscape. And I strenuously recommend against going there. There is a pinhole sound source in the cave, and if you go there at night — which you should not, which you definitely should not — what comes through is an audio-lucida causing you dreams — I am not saying they will be good dreams and I am not saying they will be bad dreams — that will not end for a very long time."

The other and I walked away. "Don't," I said when the other looked over her shoulder.

She and I walked the path more slowly than at any other time. We listened to her sister scraping and brooming a large old branch over the area immediately around her tent opening. I had taught her: that step should be a smooth one; as much as possible, gently make the first move to the outside soundscape and the last move to the inside soundscape — gently, so that all you are hearing and have heard is not forgotten.

Not fifty yards from her, behind a hummock of oak and hemlock deadfall and a bumpy apron of spongy humus, we found an area where we could camp and vaguely hear her and, when we wished, could observe her and all the while be protected quite absolutely from her discovery of us.

The early-June sun spotlighted and hammered smooth the flat area upon which we pitched our tent. The sun was bright enough that it transilluminated the child's ears.

*

(In early June now I make a little pilgrimage there, I lie down in that solar pool, and I am sure I can feel your slender arms close sleepily around my calves and thighs.)

*

I said, "We will see her later."

"She won't see us, Pea."

"She will not."

"Is that a good idea?" she asked.

Samantha Peabody aspired to never reply to impertinent questions, no matter how appropriate.

The other's butt and legs were outside our tent. Inside, she made arrangements for a nap. In a tonal ventriloquation of her gray-mother's lawyer-voice, she mumbled something, an inaudible scramble that I later translated: "Are we safe with you?" Three sharp points tacked down the sentence: *Are . . . safe . . . you?*

Inside our tent I pulled out my B♭ and sat up and practiced "Chilly Jordan," rolling from my right embouchure across a pull-off chord to my left embouchure. I wanted the simple two-punch gospel groove Huge had tried to teach me. The child put her head in my lap and rustled and flattened her body more or less under my legs, like a transitive insect under a stone. When I raised my knees a little to help, they made a crunching noise. Through all the years of lessons and even at the very end, Huge said, "Don't play so many damn notes." I think he felt lucky to be able to make me laugh. He laughed, too. I had a bad sense of tempo and a worse sense of single-note articulation, but my incorrigible offense was that I played too many notes, no matter whether I played slow blues or shuffle blues or boogie.

I would say to him, "The problem is, I hear so many notes when I'm there — inside music." This made him frown. He had taught me all those years, and I had progressed so little.

The other trembled in her sleep. Her left hand had emerged from between my thighs. I closed her hand and watched her fingers unfold.

It is not a major drama in one's life to be a serious failure as an amateur musician who has never performed for anyone but captive children, and I understand that. I am an amateur, but I practice approximately fifteen hours a week; in the worst of the winter season I practice twenty hours a week. I play fewer notes now. I can make a single note stain the whole phrase. My boots hammer my homemade stomp-board and I lose tempo less often. I keep my music chops so that when I listen to these woods I hear the sounds of their in-breath and their out-breath through my own. Out there is a noisesome world where my sister Elaine and Robert's sister Amelia and his brother Tim and Tim's children Thomas and Frida live, and where my parents lived. And Robert.

Out there I was so much more alone than here. I had had no significant teachers in my life except for Huge. I had few friends and, after divorce, almost none, and for that I have to take the full blame.

Huge had been my one friend out there.

Out there the two, adults now, live far away from their gray-mother, visiting her infrequently.

✳

(Far enough away? Infrequent enough?)

⁎

A vine whipped over the roof of the tent and a bird-cry sound rejoiced the other awake.

"Hmm?" she asked.

I said, "Maybe an early swift."

Before her eyes were fully awake, she said, "Are we going to see Betty?"

We listened first. The long vine swooped and whacked the top of our nylon tent, and whacked again, harder, an inexplicable match-strike warning sound.

⁎

(You!

I only just now, here, at this moment, have realized it was you in an act of counting coup. You striking the roof over the other and me.

There is only this one copy of the album; I picture the two of you looking into the dark pool of this together.

And now your sister knows: You.)

⁎

I asked the other to drink water before we left the tent with our magnifiers.

When we found the millipedes, we put the hand lenses away. I picked a large one up by the midsection. We could hear how its body gummed its own accordion frame. The millipede produced a stink-sound, a cha-puff.

In the most admiring way, she said, "Gross."

I said, "Don't kiss it."

She said, "Right."

"We were not going to kiss QweT-Tek-Ket," I said. "Were we?" I gave her the millipede. Jackknifing from her grip into a tussock at her feet, it left a stench on her fingertips.

"No."

"Certainly not," I said.

"You were going to kiss him, Pea."

"Certainly not."

She was firm with me: "You *were*."

I asked, "Does War still come around?"

She looked away. She did not like to be suddenly asked about her mother or about War. I felt that the only way to ask was with suddenness.

We heard a hen grouse call from a patch of ferns. I waited. "Wuk wuk," she called in order to bring her chicks near. *"Wuk wuk — wuk wuk."*

"War has money."

"I assume he has lots of that," I said. A corrupt judge has "alternative funding" from many sources; a corrupt lawyer has many corrupt judges upon whom to depend: no tree, no seed, no worm, no fish, no bird has ever participated in such an ecology.

Warren has motives. I will never know them.

In this, my album, my ecological system, I am not a storyteller accounting for the triumph of the hemlock over the wooly adelgid, the wooly adelgid over the hemlock. I am a scientist-storyteller (a failing scientist-storyteller) preoccupied with a reject-the-premise and reject-the-concept examination of paradox in forces of nature. All observable narratives of life-killing human evil and all life-giving narratives of human expiation remind me to be wary of supposing that either narrative should be eliminated.

She wished to move on. She said, "I want to talk to her."

"Go ahead." I pointed her in the general direction of her sister.

"Betty," she said. She thought she might be heard since her sister's camp was actually near.

"Go ahead. You have a small voice. Make it bigger. Go ahead."

She raised her chin and asked, "Betty?"

"Go ahead."

Her eyes wet, she pulled back her shoulders. "Betty! Betty!"

"And?"

"Betty!"

"And?" I did not stand near her. From a distance, I stabbed that word _And_ at her.

As slowly and awkwardly as a very old woman, she lowered herself to the ground. She sat, looked around her at the ferns from which the chicks had emerged. If she could, if they had stayed, she would tell them what she was feeling that caused her tears. If her mother were there, she would not tell any of this. If her sister were there, she could at least have help in telling.

What she had was Samantha Peabody. And now Samantha Peabody went to her, kneeled down to hold her.

*

The child told me how the judge paid their regular babysitter, a woman named Mrs. Preibus, to let him visit so that he could talk with them. He paid her right in front of them. Mrs. Preibus was allowed to stay during his three visits, but was paid — in cash — to keep the visits secret, during which the judge instructed the children to bring him specific items from the unlocked file boxes in their mother's apartment study.

She said he wore one pair of glasses when he came there, and another smaller pair when he examined the documents.

When they brought him the items, they were instructed that they must say, "Look what I have brought you" or "I want you to see this," before handing them over.

He would look at them, take notes; a few times, he took pictures of the pages. He would give the files back to the one and the other, who would return them to their proper places. During the months of April and May he evidently paid Mrs. Preibus as his accomplice; before his visits, she helped them practice: "Look what I have brought you" and "I want you to see this."

He told them that Mrs. Preibus had witnessed the terrible beatings, she had witnessed some of the worst of the beatings, though the children knew there had only ever been the one episode of hitting and that there had been no beatings.

He told them that he was paying Mrs. Preibus to protect them, that was a good thing wasn't it? Yet the children clearly understood that no harm would come to them except from him and Mrs. Preibus.

On his very last visit the second week in May, he asked them for nothing. He had done so much for them, he said, he had done everything he could do to protect them from the beatings.

For two months he visited.

He planted.

He planted.

With precise extortive effort Mrs. Preibus also planted and planted. She planted everything he asked. She and the judge obviously believed that if they repeatedly told the children they had experienced many beatings, that they had endured many more than they would ever possibly remember, they would come to believe this. False memory is that much more posible to induce in attentive, facile young minds. I have firsthand knowledge of it.

He told the children they must remember that they had offered him information he had not sought, that they had said to him,

"Look what I have brought you" and "I want you to see this."

They knew, he said, that what was in the files was horrible; their mother had committed offenses against other people and other people's children, acts almost as terrible as beating children. He hoped they understood that the information would be the essential evidence for taking them from their mother, for putting her in prison, and that is where she would go the very day they ever told anyone about his visits.

He told them that they were adopted, that their own real mother was dead and their own real father unknown. He told them their mother kept that a secret, and he asked them why they thought she would keep that secret.

He did not sink the knives deeper; he withdrew them.

He said that he and Mrs. Preibus had never met. Did the children understand that he and Mrs. Preibus had never met — because there had never been a "Mrs. Preibus" at all? If anyone ever asked, they must say that there had never been a Mrs. Preibus. If their mother insisted there had been such a person, no matter what the circumstance they must say that their mother was mistaken.

After that last visit from War, Mrs. Preibus did not return. Without offering Mrs. Preibus a second chance, their mother hired another babysitter.

They did not tell their mother they knew about her adoption of them. They were not certain he had told them the truth, though they felt that it must be the truth, something made them feel that it must.

*

All of this spilled from the other, who rubbed her eyes and face with her stinking fingers. When she realized that she was not inside a volcano but was inside my embrace there where we sat on the ground, she sank her full weight into me so deeply that I felt my own weeping was hers.

She ran out of tears and, after a while, I did too. She stood. She helped me up.

"My face is smelly," she said, drying stains from her glasses.

"There was a lot of stink on that millipede." I remembered that this species of marshland and meadow millipede often kept company in that particular season with fireflies. I said, "Tonight we will visit here on our way back from our night observation of your sister."

What a shame that she had only Samantha Peabody. She needed someone who was more sensitive to little things six years old. I asked, "Could we talk about this again? Could we talk about this — your mother and all of it — again, and a lot more times, and then whenever you want?"

She said, "I'm hungry," which was a more encouraging answer than none.

Together we washed the odor from her the best we could. My rough hands pumiced her hands and her arms. "You, Janet, should have stopped pinching millipedes years ago." I dried Janet with my neck scarf.

We ate crackers with pretend butter spread to the edges. We

drank cool water we had just filtered from the stream. Impossibly, the turkey jerky caused us slobbery smiles.

In all my efforts to make the two children merely valued specimens I failed.

"More?" Janet asked, already spreading pretend butter to the edges of a cracker for me. To this day, I believe she would have offered me the cracker even if it was all the food she had or could ever have.

Janet, my youngest. I thought of her now as my own daughter.

٭

Before dusk, without need of binoculars, we observed Betty, my oldest, rocking her legs and bare feet on the bur pine branch just above her tent. She was in a listening perch.

We both made the effort to hear what she heard. Something below her: skunks and rabbits moving cautiously, grubbing and chewing but twitching from fearful alertness; grasshoppers sawing at themselves, hitting more flats than sharps, and all at once going off like mines. Something beyond her and well beyond us: the woofings of a bear and of bear cubs; the hundred servile creatures giving specific, encoded sonic responses for the sake of discriminate warnings in their territories. Something all around: the throngs of terrestrial and aquatic insects attuned to the encasings they had worn, to the flowing water currents spitting them up into the reaching air that dried their new and already dying skin. When we humans have lost the last notes of this earth's singing, we will have lost all evidence of it in each other's voices. Only human saying will be possible, only human noise will exist. When nature is gone from human nature, everything sacred our hearing once experienced will be replaced by maddening deafness.

I said, "This is a good time. The cave. Are you ready for the cave?"

We belly-crawled into the cave mouth, which was approximately ten meters from the cave's other mouth. When we were inside, Janet stood up, and I hunched under the muciferous ceiling.

The two curved cave chambers were the head and tail of an S shape. When we reached the center, fairly large brittle bones snapped under us, and we had to boot-scoot to avoid repeating that desiccative crunching sound. I knew they were animal bones, but I only recently learned how they came to be there, how various CCC projects and commercial operations had brought their donkeys and mules to such caves because that was easier than digging holes to bury them. All along the Appalachian range where tunnels and trail systems and mining and logging operations had worked these animal slaves to death there followed ghost stories of cave mouths braying child cries. The old ones taught their children: "If you wanna hear more of that infernal racket, call out, 'Lazy Jenny, Lazy Jack, lazy, lazy front to back.' The ghosts come out! If you want it quiet, say, 'Here's the water, here's the food, here the halter, here the load.'"

I held a small penlight that was helpful since it made my hand a point of orientation for us. I knew the cave well, and I knew at this point we were two or three steps from the curve and only a dozen more steps from the cave's other mouth. Janet whispered, "She won't hear us? See us?"

I said, "We will be invisible and inaudible," though I had my doubts.

We followed the curve. A few seconds of sonorous imminence made me aware of the cave of my own body and the smaller cave of hers. I could hear. The mouth of the earth pressed to the mouth of the cave, and a child's voice sounded and resounded there.

The best I could tell, Betty was in front of her tent and was singing. She might have been singing long phrases of happy sighing. She might have been singing in excited self-conversation.

Hearing her sister's voice made Janet giggle, and she nudged herself against me like I was a favorite scratching post or an imaginary scraggy companion.

We listened to her timbre change from bright to silk-bright, from lifting to lifting off, to flying. There were landings in her voice but they were touch-landings, and so we could hear one motionless word — *me . . . me* — but with none of the words still moving and lifting *me* away. Making everything resonant and nothing evident: that was the nature of Betty's sonic beauty.

I could have listened to her forever.

I thought she might be singing "Temperature." I thought she might be answering the eeemeeemmm-mmm-EEE of the myriad acclamations in the woods. It was supreme sound. Ablaze.

I sometimes wonder whether she has ever again known that feeling-oneself-feel solitude.

*

(Have you?)

*

Her voice was loud and then fearless-loud as she danced toward the mouth of the cave and danced away. Her voice, not evasive, implicitly asked, *Hunt me*, asked, Find me.

We could not see her, but we could hear her scrambling feet and, strangely, her swerving and swooping body.

Her arms-outreached silhouette came into view at the mouth of the cave. Preposterously large.

The giant creature stood under the streaming cold water. She vibrated like the struck steel rod of a kaleidophone. She contracted into a smaller and more ominous form, bent head and neck shuddering. Then: unmoving as an owl.

She scampered in under the cave's lip. She was eight strides away from us, but because of the depth of field affecting us, she disappeared from our view.

The laughter sound could have come from the woods, from the splashing creek, but seemed to come from her.

"Hello," she said to the ghosts in the cave, said to the cave, said to the heavily breathing presences in the cave, said to her shadow form.

And who does not wish to enter one of the places of her own dreams where she can greet the foretelling harmonic form of herself?

"I'm here," she said.

I do not know if she was looking at us, though she peered right at Janet and me, two dark uncertain occurrences.

I imagined that she turned her left ear toward us.

Her feet skittered without moving back or forward. She was trying to hold herself there without offering herself to us.

My weight shifted downward and my lungs filled up in such a way that I thought my back and buttocks were going to float against the cave ceiling. I realized that my penlight was still on, that the large creature was staring at my penlight but apparently could not see the hand holding it.

She unfolded her wings — zzzss-zzza! sza! ssszzza! came from somewhere inside — outside — and she stretched them out — the water splashed onto her with toy-piano plinking sounds — and she turned so that we could hear the feathery darknesses held behind her and aloft — her whispered, mummified "Bye" — our hearts like bells shaking off snow — I am sure she flew and did not walk away.

We heard her remove the pine branches she had attached to her arms.

We heard her enter her tent where she was still wildly carrying on when we retreated, crawled out, walked back through plainchant veils of fireflies to our campsite, silent.

July 2 – 8, 2004

Carla was an hour late in bringing Betty and Janet to me.

＊

(Betty.

Janet.

For the nine months from October 2003 to June 2004, I had fought with myself about you, my "two," my "one" and "other." I had wanted to preserve my distance and so I kept the naming of you absolutely impersonal — until Janet's tears, until Betty's wild cave dance.

Fa.

So.

La.

My heart had given way that swiftly.)

＊

I sat under a young poplar, its lower branches responding to the breeze by waltzing with the branches of another poplar about the same age. The trees made the dancers' frame that steadies and lightens their torsos, and lifts the dancers' hearts toward each other but keeps them apart and defines one who leads and one who harmonizes the movements.

I closed my eyes in order to hear the sun rise in the rustling arms.

The first mist-light dissolves rapidly in these woods in July, but on that day the light was sustained enough to penetrate my closed lids, to fool me. I could not be sure I heard how the blooms of sound invaginated in the forest mist were rapidly evaginating.

The diminishing volume reached total compression. At the point when the silence trembled, eversion of sound began: the burring of mud daubers and yellow jackets and paper wasps in different folds and upon different stone and earthen and wooden faces; the birds, less vocal than in May and June, hitting their wings against their chests and heads, their backs and bellies; the straining sounds of splitting, unsheathing, shedding, gagging and downgulping that are the sounds of toadskin splitting across the toad's back and the toad straining to unglove itself all in one piece and then wadding its pale other into its mouth where it must dissolve in order to go down.

Janet and Betty and Carla — and my sister Elaine — arrived in Carla's shining behemoth automobile.

I stayed sitting, and Elaine stood over me, asking did I believe I could just avoid her forever — did I think my return letters that were nothing more than barely friendly postcards were enough — did I understand that the girls were weirded out by me — that Carla was concerned about leaving the girls with me — did

I think about how awfully eccentric I would be after another few months with no contact with the girls or with Carla — or with her? Sam, Sam, Elaine told me, do you think it's understandable, the whole crawling-down-in-a-hole life — did you feel like you should tell Carla who the hell this butch-bitch-hick-horror-story Drummer was that you made Betty visit?

Elaine wanted to know did I need help because if I did then there was a good psychologist in Asheville who specialized in the Whatever Disorder was my disorder — did I — did I —

I could see Carla sitting inside the car, looking very sadly at me, both her hands at twelve o'clock on the wheel.

— did I want to know did I ever want to know anything about my own sister and her new husband — pretty new anyway — was I too self-absorbed for that? Elaine said, Have I said this — I guess I have — my husband is old before his time — did I did I —

Janet smiled at me and Betty smiled at me through the closed car window, Betty's head atop Janet's. Their bobs were newly groomed so that their hair, unnaturally adult in appearance, was also unnaturally alike. Who did the two adopted children favor?

By serendipitous accident they favored me in their manner of tilting their heads a certain asking way toward the world's resounding woods, of speaking softly, of holding inside silence, of not bleating.

※

(You have not become bleaters, I trust.)

※

Elaine wanted to know did I actually have any idea what Carla was going through with Judge Warren making her life hell, extorting money from her in stages — did I have information because if I had information, something the girls had told me that Carla ought to know, then I had better tell because Carla and she were friends who came through for each other — did I —

Carla could not see that Janet and Betty were ready to burst from the car and come to me.

— Did you ever ever ever have a friend a real friend ever, did you, well, probably not, not even back to grade school — except for Robert who was — really was — did I want to know what his last words were — the last?

Elaine said, He told me he *should* die, that it was the right shit to happen to him — for fucking Carla — for fucking that fucking Carla — that fucking husband-fucker Carla.

His last words, she said. Did you ever wonder, Sam? — you did — I know you — and I know you did.

And she asked did I know Carla was just about the best friend Elaine had back then — well, has now — the best one for almost fifty years. She asked did I know that Carla told her everything — did I — did I know that Carla's children did not like Elaine but that Carla still told her everything?

Elaine sucked in air.

Barely aware of her own spilling, she had spilled out something that she had definitely never intended.

She heard the words splash into me.

She would have gone right on talking but she heard the splashing. And had I heard? That is what she wondered.

I had.

Hearing the pleuritic microtonal shift of her voice into guilt, I felt more pity for her than for me. I have trained my hearing to drink and to chew human speech, to take in the ground glass and the unbroken crystal goblet of the phonemic soundscape. I am not exaggerating when I say that I have heard ripples across the skin and ridge and wrinkle of space-time. Am I supposed to demur about the fact that I have heard beyond so-called normal human hearing?

*

(Why would I wish for you two to read this? I am never sure I am writing this for you. For you I take things out, for me I put things in.

There is less here than I meant.

There is more here than I mean.)

*

Elaine had said, *"Fucking Carla,"* as if saying Carla's name and surname. But that made no sense.

I did the kind of calculation a brown thrasher might do in the act of anting, when the bird flails at an anthill, beak to tail, inviting the ants to swarm over its body.

According to Elaine, as his dying words, Robert had said something like "That fucking Carla"? *His last words.*

Elaine had blurted out his last words. She had known all that time, and I had not known until that very moment: the person with whom Robert betrayed me was Carla, graymother to Janet and Betty; Carla, old friend to Robert and his sister and my sister.

I wondered, Did I ever imagine that?

I had imagined.

*

At one of our early "divorce strategy meetings" in The Baker's Dozen coffeehouse in West Asheville, Carla had told me a little story about how she decided never to become a trial lawyer once she learned in law school how juries were selected. She said that defense counsel and prosecution counsel intentionally and with only rare exception preferred ignorant jurors: uneducated and passive and shallow thinkers; well educated and aggressive and arrogant and lazy in their thinking; uneducated and educated elderly women and men marked in their speech and even in their facial expressions and gestures by a grudge that sealed their minds shut.

Carla had adjusted herself inside her presentment, the way a person shifts her foot in her expensive shoe. "In voir dire you and opposing counsel compete to put ignorant people on a jury," Carla had said. I must have looked at her with disbelief. She said, "You didn't know that there is a Punishment System but that there is no such thing as a Justice System, did you?"

She'd said, "I wished I could never commit injustice. God, I wished I could never do that." She laughed the way a person laughs at tragedies in which she has chosen to be the central player.

And we schemed to eviscerate Robert. We shared an almond croissant, and one of us asked why bakers always put too much powdered sugar on an almond croissant. We agreed: overkill.

❊

Carla's little explanation about voir dire had quietly, pleasurably landed in me then, splashed into me with the identical sudden plangency of the needle now hitting the vinyl in my sister Elaine's voice.

I asked Elaine, "Would you bring Carla and Betty and Janet from the car?"

Elaine wished to know why. She asked whether it wouldn't be best for everyone to stay in the car, for her to return to the car, for everything to be the way it was.

She dropped to her knees.

And she did the crying for me.

I did not hold her while she cried over the situation in which she was trapped.

Inside the car, Carla observed Elaine's crying. She made a gesture to her children to go to me, but they stayed where they were in the back seat. Carla rested her chin on her hands in insincere prayer.

Elaine heaved and cried and mutter-cried, her arms reaching for me. I let her crying go on. How could I not let her go on? I loved my sister — I loved the paradoxes of loving my sister. Over time she had become less important in my life, a natural process of distancing that still continues. She is someone I once knew who competed with me for food and attention and space in the family nest. Young humans desire neither to stay in nor to return to such civilized confinement. When we had flown away from that nest Elaine and I rarely sought each other's company again. Nothing had brought us together in the way that Robert's nephew and niece had once, at least briefly, renewed the connection between him and his brother Tim.

Elaine was so weakened now she could hardly stand. I did not and do not feel as close a connection with her as I felt at that time with Betty and Janet whom I'd known for ten weeks. I understood that the long friendship between Elaine and Robert and Carla and Robert's sister Amelia went deeper than the friendship between Elaine and me. I understood that her tears were for them and for herself. I felt love called out of me for all of them and for me. I would not be honest if I said that I felt love for her alone.

"What? What?" Carla asked, the two not following her out of the car. "What?"

"You and Robert," I said.

As I sit here now, words come that wouldn't come then: *You and Robert fucked each other. And congratulations to you for that. And congratulations for keeping the secret, Carla. And lucky you that Robert kept the secret, too, to the lip of the grave. And what could I do now except throw some dirt on that old coffin full of shit?*

Carla pushed Elaine back onto her knees. On the verge of striking her, she said, "You —"

"I told." Poor Elaine, brain-deaf and stupid and a stranger to me, poor Elaine, a deaf and deafening stranger, sobbed, poor Elaine who never heard or thought or felt anything she didn't sooner or later tell.

"You told *Elaine?*" I asked Carla.

Unmoving as a stone statue, Carla said, "An accident. The time with him was nothing like what you think." She spoke coldly.

The words didn't come to me then. But now I want to say: *You're talking about you and Robert, and all of it. So. So it went on for an all-of-it time, then, and so it wasn't a one-time fuck, it was an "accident" and then a second accident and a set of accidents and a pattern of accidents that were probably also going on around the time just before the end of him.*

Janet and Betty gazed out of the car at this whole absurd scene. They did not leave the car. They did not roll down the windows. I formed the impression that only one part of this interested them: Samantha with two women she could not help in any way; Samantha looking back at Janet and Betty, not finding the words for what she would say.

*

Everyone agreed with me that the five of us should go up the trail together and that Elaine and Carla should stay at the campsite until the next morning. Though they had consented, some doubt registered on the faces of Betty and Janet, and I said, "We are making the kind of terrible choice a group entity of humans will make at the time of an unprecedented disturbance."

Janet said, "You made that up. You just make things up and they sound good but you made them up."

Betty said, "Janet's right."

Elaine, her eyes and nose still watering, muttered about cursing and about adults making mistakes and children understanding adults' mistakes later in their lives, and, and, and … and as Carla locked up her car, Elaine said, "It's a long way," and asked, "Should we have food — does anyone have food with them? — Carla, any food? — I have Skittles but not many are left — and half of a Snickers — we'll get hungry — do you have food in the car? — Carla, listen to me — Sam feeds them almost nothing, you know — Carla? Carla?" She took Carla's hand.

Carla said, "I have antacid and Slim Jims. I have —"

Elaine remembered that she also had Fig Newtons, an unopened large package, in her shoulder-bag purse thing. A snacker all her life, she would keep things in there like a family-size bag of salt-water taffy, and Fritos, Nutella, a plastic table knife, a spork, a 16-ounce bottled water.

"I have — Thin Mints — and —"

I asked Carla to put her Slim Jims in Elaine's bag. I was convinced Elaine's buzzsaw-talking would deter any curious, hungry animals.

Rummaging for the Slim Jims, Carla said, "I had some chocolate-covered pretzels — I ate them though."

"Carla," I said, "you are a monster."

On the trail, Betty walked on my right, Janet on my left. They were dressed like Samantha Peabody. Their confident, striding walk was mine.

The wind picked up and sheared off and made shape notes in a singing school, the surrounding mountains dividing up the tenor, treble, bass, and alto parts. Betty and Janet had trouble with their full packs, so we adjusted and readjusted them. I suspected new books were being smuggled in, and I asked whether we should unload and rebalance the packs. "No" was the firm answer from Janet, then more firm yet from Betty. I said, "I have a question for you," and, receiving no response, I said, "Here is my question: Are you intelligent? Or are you brave?" I offered no choice for them to be both brave and intelligent.

"Intelligent," said Betty trying to obey the established sonic adventure rule of responding swiftly to my questions.

"Not brave?" I asked.

"Intelligent," she said.

I watched Janet square herself when I asked, "And you?"

She scowled almost indiscernibly at Betty as if her sister should answer for her.

Betty looked over her shoulder in order to fix her mother in place and, so, to forget her.

Janet smiled at me, a gnome smile that was specific to the two of us. I am you, my simulacrum seemed to say. I am you and I have come to meet you.

"Intelligent," I answered for her. She nodded yes.

We walked.

Elaine continued to drone. Did I — did I —

Three strides behind her, Carla had given up hearing Elaine or us.

I said, "Neither of you is brave enough to inspire the other to be ignorant, I suppose."

"I suppose," said Janet.

For another half hour, we did not look behind us at Carla or Elaine until we came to the campsite where, without their help, we set up a second tent close to my tent, close enough that we could hear them in their tent and they could hear us in ours. Before everyone arrived I had retrieved this second tent and other equipment from a cache box buried at the place that is now one of my seasonal camps.

Janet asked, "Who stays where?"

"They'll be here just for one night," I said. "They're going back in the morning."

Betty said, "Good."

"Who stays where?" asked Janet.

I said, "Listen, Carla, you understand — right? — that I cannot be in the same tent with you?"

She said, "I —"

"Betty and Janet and I will be together. The extra tent will be yours and Elaine's for the night. You've got a fancy, roomy set-up."

I asked Betty and Janet to take our new food supply and Elaine's added junk food to the storage canister. They left; the moment they felt, mistakenly, that they were out of my eyesight, they filched from the package of Skittles.

I brought Elaine and Carla inside their own tent and oriented them to the arrangement, which included mats and sheets and a powerful flashlight (with small carabiner attached) for each of them. "Just call me for what you want. My tent is practically on top of yours. You cannot keep food in here," I said firmly, "absolutely none." I warned them to take the flashlight if either of them left the tent. I said, "You can get lost easily, or fall," and inside me I asked Carla, *Isn't it easy to fall, to commit injustice, to practice law as a crime to which you make others an accessory?* I entered another chamber of riddle: *So. When we were drawing and quartering Robert, at the point he was most helpless, at the point you were still seducing him and tending to him even in the hospital, what were you telling him? He would not have asked why you were doing this to him because he would have felt — right? — he would have felt the whole mess was as it should be, that he was getting what he deserved. But what were you telling him? "I'm proceeding exactly as Sam asks me to proceed." Was that what you said? "Sam. Sam gives me my orders." Was that it?*

I said, "Do not come to my tent, no matter what. This is Betty and Janet's sonic adventure, not yours. I do not permit interference here."

Elaine said, "You are weird, Sam — see what I mean about how weird you are getting — well — more weird than ever: 'I do not permit interference here.' That's — it's something you don't tell their mother — who talks that way? — it's — what? — inside you are you writing out what you say before you speak it? — it sounds just like that — it —"

"I understand," said Carla.

"I'm going to get out of here," said Elaine as she unzipped the front panel and, in defiance of me, went to my tent.

"I understand," said Carla, only the two of us now left in her tent, a structure as perfectly sealed and tight as a water bubble but easily penetrated by sound. The skin luffed hard, an unusual blast. I said, "The wind hits in July. And August and —" and a whistling punch came again. "See?"

"You've been good to Betty and Janet."

"They love me."

Carla said, "They love you. They really do and they want to be lost with you, which is a deep kind of love. And they can never get enough of you. From one adventure to another, they talk and talk about you."

Actually, she only said, "They do." She did not say, "They love you" or any of the rest of that. She did not break down and pour out an apology. No suppliant, tearful words. I have written Carla's fictional apology (a full account, six album pages), and I have removed those pages. Some album items, the falsest, I have kept as overplus, the set-aside pages that stay nearby and whisper to the pages that remain.

There is one particular false account I have written that I keep tucking into and removing from the album. The well-crafted passage ends this way: "I felt so bad," said Carla. "I felt so bad that I couldn't undo it all, that I couldn't make it up to you. Or to myself. I felt so bad, I wanted to bring you something. I did.

You can see. I did. I brought you my children."

Carla sat down, and I sat down across from her. She did not need to apologize since her shame and grief darkened and dampened the inside of this nylon bubble, which took another wallop from the wind.

"Christ!" said Elaine, her voice crosswise with the voice of the shaking trees. "Should I come back there?"

"You think you would be safe in here?" I asked, which caused me to chugiggle and caused Carla to gichuckle. The acoustics of the tent made our vocalizations sound chirruping.

We heard Betty and Janet return to the campsite. We were aware that they would be standing outside, listening, waiting for Elaine to leave the tent meant for Betty and Janet and me.

At this time of year, the next-to-last intermittent sounds diminish in the woods. The sounds cause every creature here to hurry, to begin singing our last, and to bury our secret dormant truths where they will best hatch, and where we will shiver in the frost and will wear our frozenness to our deaths.

Neither Carla nor I had words. The encasing silence had utterly silenced even our bodies, and it was now a matter of time until what emerged from her was me, what emerged from me was her. All the secrets — a person resists their abnormal presence by growing a gall around them, a place where the secrets can live before they click and buzz their way out.

"I have always liked gall lore," I told Carla.

"Okay," she said, helplessly.

At the time it did not occur to me that gall lore might not matter to her, a person who liked things to matter.

I told her, "That — gall lore — is the kind of lesson I teach Betty and Janet in our adventures. A gall is a kind of amplifier attached to a tree; the three of us go from one to another tree; we listen."

"Betty and Janet told me you called them 'the one' and 'the other.'"

"Well. I —"

"They like it," she said, shifting her position, newly aware that her untoughened rump could not adjust to the cold floor.

"I stopped calling them that in June. The June adventure was heavy."

"'Heavy'?"

"Really heavy, Carla."

"They liked it, Sam. They needed it, I can tell you that. You know: CDCJ." Did she really believe that Betty and Janet, keenly listening in on our conversation, would not know her shorthand for Warren, Chief District Court Judge?

I said, "They're not mine. They're not at all mine. I wished for children. After my body kept putting out the little fires Robert and I made, we gave up. We gave up, then — then I did not wish for children — until these two." She tilted her chin down, her mouth open, three notes of out-breath and one forehearable note of in-breath.

I asked, "Did Robert tell Amelia?"

"She knew."

"When?" I asked.

During the past twelve years there has been time for me to follow the hard and the faint evidence, to calculate and recalculate the order of events: Robert and Carla fucking in 1993, probably the first incident at the time of my parents' deaths; fucking in 1993 and 1997, fucking not so often since she was a single graymother with two in diapers, but fucking often enough for her to fuck her way out of terrible episodes of feeling depressed and overwhelmed. The affair was over by 1997 when he told Amelia and Elaine the name of "the woman" and when he confessed to me about "the woman" he would not name. I had asked him, "Why?" And when he started to give his reasons — that he loved me and loved me with the all of him — that he fucked "the woman," but that he understood he was a convenient tool for her — that he always thought of me as a person who was alone, essentially alone and had been, and who was always setting out to be more alone — I asked what I had meant to ask: "Why did you tell me about her?"

And I did not ask, "Who is she?"

And I already understood that he felt his adultery had been so dishonorable and so disrespectful of me he could only regain some sense of himself as honorable and respectful if he confessed. He invited upon himself the furious mercilessness he knew he deserved. In love with me, not done with being in love with me, he understood exactly what I would do: I would make myself more alone by destroying him. Eliminating him from my life while still in love with him: I had perfected the practice of this every day of our twenty-nine years together.

I'm confident that my calculations are correct. During the divorce arrangements he and Carla resumed fucking each other. A dangerous thrill for her. And for him? A way to commit to dying outside marriage and not simply to continue dying inside marriage.

A gall, I offered (unbidden), is often a world created by insects, aphids and beetles and flies and wasps agitating a plant into forming a boil of intensifying and then teeming sound. You listen to the thrumming coming from that strange goblin-mouth on a tree — and who knows what will come out? The guests, the creatures called "inquilines," have laid their eggs there. "Gall lore," I said, "is one story after another about the unimaginable singing guests for which you did not ask."

She said, "You just do and say what you want, am I right?"

If I could have had words, I could have said to her, "And you? You just say and do what you want, am I wrong?"

She glared at me on my way out, and said, "You sent Betty on a hike alone where she could have gotten lost."

"I lose them," I said. "That's what you pay me for. Now you — get lost."

The children, once more in my tent, attached themselves to my legs. I said, "You've been listening."

"Duh," said Janet. "Duh," said Betty.

From inside the other tent, Carla said loud enough for me to hear, "You scared Janet half to death, sending Betty off like that."

As if oblivious of Carla's company, Elaine still went on and on like a field cricket. Betty and Janet had not put in their P-A devices in order to block Elaine out, but they had learned how to select out certain sounds.

I said to Carla, "Oh. I did scare her. I wish I hadn't. I did. And she loves her older sister — like a mother."

Carla said, "You sent Betty to the old woman's cabin, to the Drummer, and you made her stay a whole night there — what were you thinking? — the whole night."

"Mansour Cove — a place where you can hear in the way the first humans heard the everywhere and the nowhere. And she probably slept with the old lesbian," I said. "Think of that! Drummer has a dish-stone at the head of her bed. She hasn't exactly secured it as she should. The stone is blood red and seems like it could fall and crush your skull at any moment."

"This is not a joking matter," said Carla. "The poor thing —"

"—is alone, drinks, reads the Psalms, masturbates, rolls her own, has not a single inhibition of any kind."

Carla was not finished. "Betty showed me a picture, and she said, 'I knew I had seen it before!' and she laughed harder and better than I'll ever see her laugh again."

She showed her mother a *picture*? I could not help but ask about the picture, and Betty explained that Drummer's home was not at all like the witch's home in her illustrated edition of *Hansel & Gretel*, but that it had been better to show her mother the illustration and to tell her what Drummer's home was like than to try to explain. "Mom's impatient," Betty said, and Janet chimed in, "She doesn't want to hear."

"*I am not!*" came their mother's voice from inside the interference of Elaine's voice.

Elaine, ignoring Carla there in the tent with her, blithered on and on.

Betty and Janet were sorry for what they had said, especially sorry we had heard their words. But they were not sorry to be separate from Elaine and their mother.

We waited. The wind rattled the hollow plastic ribs of the tents in a whu-whu-whoosh of wings rapidly opened and closed against feathered bodies.

"I do want to hear," Carla said, "I'm impatient but —"

Elaine, who had not heard her, who had not heard herself, who had not heard Betty or Janet, said, "Why in the first place would you give them to Sam that's what I can't figure out — jesuschrist — her of all people a week at a time up here with bears and crazy drumming bitches and what-have-yous hunters mountain in-bred Klanners — with weather that beats you with floods with storms with no television with no books — she won't let them have books! — with bugs that sting bite throw stink on you with practically no food with …"

I asked, "Do you need to water the garden, Elaine?" I had to ask twice. I said, "The daylight leaves fast."

"…with her awful harmonica her awfuler singing with binoculars she won't let them use with rules she makes up on the spot … with … I — I — okay okay."

We heard Elaine tramp upriver to the latrines.

Carla laughed. Something about Elaine's tramping was humorous, it was, and Carla's laughter gave Betty and Janet permission to laugh. Carla asked, "Are you two obeying Sam?" And, "You are?" And, "If so, why?" And, after the last falling inflections of silence, "Can I come over to your tent?"

"No!" we all three said.

I asked Betty if Drummer had let her see her scar.

Janet sounded the word. Scar.

Betty said, "Yep."

Inside *Yep* I could hear the resonating timbre of *Scar. No. If so. You two. Okay. Do you. I do*: the continued existence of sound — so much polarizing and attracting echoing in one small chamber of time's vast caverns.

"And?" asked Carla. "And?" asked Janet.

Betty said, "Drummer goes around naked at night." I knew this was true. "She's got an ankle scar. Scary. Scary, like it shouldn't be on her."

It should be, I thought. The scar should be on her, a good mark.

"The scar's got a story," said Betty, and didn't offer more. Instead, she said, "Drummer has a toilet bucket like cats use. Out on her porch. I dumped it for her."

"That was certainly kind of you," I said.

"Quite kind," said Janet, with coldness enough to demand the scar story.

"The bucket was making me sick. Like — really." She said, "The porch creaks and you don't even have to walk before sounds come up. Through the boards."

"That's not funny," said Carla's voice, somehow more crisp reaching our bubble from her bubble. "Poor hygiene is not funny."

"You have to put in the litter stuff with a little shovel." She said to her sister, "The rhodo hell? Remember? That's where she dumps the bucket."

I decided to change topics. I asked if Betty had seen Drummer's giant hundred-year-old Modern Home Grand stove. I asked if she had seen the Maria Martin painting of Audubon. Betty answered, "Drummer showed me," and I was glad to know. Maria Martin, who was John James Audubon's watercolor painter for the most significant and profitable period of his career, had made a finely detailed portrait depicting the famous man as a small bird freshly dead and mounted for study on a table draped with a woman's silk scarf as a liquid effect. Audubon was in a colorful frock and a black-fringed red-copper toque, and his bill was clamped hard shut, and his talons had been wired around a watercolor paintbrush bearing leaves autumn golden. Blood-tears brimmed in his open eyes. Glued to the leaves and slightest leaf stems — you could only see this when you looked close — were insects specific to a pond habitat. Accurate to the smallest details, they were all flattened as if between plates of glass. The background wash was something like the shimmer of a mayfly hatch over a streambed, but you could not really say; this effect was what Drummer, fluent in moonshine French, called "déjà dit," elusively familiar.

"You would have liked her place," Betty said loud enough to be heard by her mother.

"I would have liked it, too," said Janet.

"She has a rat cellar."

I said, "A root cellar."

She said, "She calls it a rat cellar."

Drummer had all of her teeth but had the problem of too many, and her pronunciation sometimes failed.

"Is she — like — okay?" asked Janet.

"She's good," Betty answered. Some experiences she wanted for herself, though her sister and she were so close they would easily forget where one ended and the other started in our compact space.

*

(Are you so close today, twelve years later? Would that be a good thing at all?

Do you think of me?

Of course you do.)

*

On my most recent encounter with Drummer six months ago, I asked her again about Betty's visit in 2004. I was not surprised to learn new information: that she had offered Betty smokes, offered her candied short-horned grasshoppers and not fresh ones, put a fox-face (gray fox) hat on her, offered her moon-shine, asked her to meet her slime mold pet Shara Wadji and to feed him oat flakes, and had kissed the freaked-out child's arms down to her fingers and had tasted all ten tips.

Betty had told Janet and me that Drummer taught her "The I Don't Song" when the child objected to smelling how the dead smelled.

*

(Am I right — was it Drummer's great-grandmother's burial shoes she put under your nose, Betty?

"That Betty," Drummer told me this March, in her best story-book voice, "I could've et her up she was such a tasty goodness!"

Drummer is now eighty-nine. Did Drummer explain to you, Betty, that when she was your age her great-grandmother's five sisters showed her how to fix a body for burial? Did she tell about how the great-grandcorpse's foot and ankle bones made cracking sounds when they were trying to put her shoes on her?)

*

In our tent on that windy July, I had asked Betty how "The I Don't Song" went. I knew she would remember, since it had so few verses. But Betty didn't share the song.

I provided some of the words: "I don't is a stubborn moth — I don't is a darn liar — anything can be done that can be done — I don't is a barn fire — burns up the barn, flies in and is gone."

Betty said she didn't remember.

I said, "Drummer learned it from Cornet Pull's mother when she lived on the unlevel and untillable land they sold to Negro hill people in the thirties."

"Is any of it true? That's what you have to wonder," said Carla, speaking from the other tent. I supposed she was addressing her children huddling against me in the tent. Or she might have been talking to only me. The wind was giving the camp a schoolmarm admonition, and Carla might have been asking her question to the higher power, which in this case was, of course, her lawyer-self.

"You were not frightened." I stated this as a fact because I knew.

Betty said, "Drummer calls you her 'own-born cousin,' Pea."

"No, no — we are lovers. (And you understand me? Drummer and I are lovers.) Drummer employs mountain expressions like 'my own-born cousin' when she is attempting to be a mountainfolk witch to a city child trying to nibble at her little house."

I asked Carla, "You have not yet taken them to Dollywood, have you?" And when she did not answer, I said, "Shame on you."

We heard Elaine tramping back into the camp, muttering as if she had not stopped doing so since she was inside the womb. When I heard her go into the tent with Carla, I asked, "So. Amelia was the other person who knew? You knew and Amelia knew about Carla and Robert."

In her legal voice Carla said, "Answer her, Elaine."

"Well," Elaine said, "Amelia hated you and Carla for what you had done to him — but she had forgiven Carla for the divorce stuff — but then when she knew about Carla and Robert — you know — *knew* about them — she could forgive Carla but not Robert — because of you or some kind of loyalty to you that made no sense at all — and she didn't really know you well but hated you after the divorce stuff — God she hated you — she never went back to the hospital after that — she ended up hating everybody — and me — and me but that makes no sense and I'm not going to dwell on that — and I guess you've never heard from her since — have you?"

I said, "Poor Amelia." Before and during and after the times she hated me, Amelia had loved me, and I had no doubt of that. Poor Amelia.

Carla said it, too. "Poor Amelia."

Elaine said, "I don't know — should we even talk about this with the children hearing?"

Betty and Janet put in their P-A devices.

They did not hear Elaine talking through the night, falling asleep, waking and talking.

I played my low D harp and sang, "The wind, the wind, the heaven-born wind — the world, the world, the hell-bound world — get home now, Pal, get home again."

"That song's so pretty," said Carla. "Like you're talking to a horse."

*

In the morning when we hiked them back to the car, a haze had settled over our path, a blue haze with sounds flowing into it from the shifting pebbles in the creek swelling with rainfall on

Little Char Knob and Jacob Mountain.

I hugged Elaine, who hugged me back too hard. Betty and Janet declined Elaine's hug, but they agreeably exchanged pats.

Carla and Betty and Janet and I quick-hugged in a clump and we separated. We weren't done with each other, so we hugged in a tighter clump. Carla started to remove from her keychain the flashlight I had given her; I asked her to keep it, and to plan on staying with Betty and Janet and me on the last night of the August adventure — and to not bring Elaine. She agreed to do that.

We waved goodbye.

The wind, E minor, had stopped straining so hard.

Betty and Janet did not seem sad at all. They were bouncy, exhilarated. They were uncontainable. On the trail, only a few strides from the trailhead, I asked them to be quiet in order to listen better. They were then more careful with their footfalls.

I asked what particulate sound they heard in the blue haze.

They did not hesitate to identify the source: a footfall that was not quite normal. They had probably been aware of that sound all night.

*

(Drummer once had a clubfoot. Betty knows this story. I am guessing that Betty has kept it to herself and that there is a very petty part of her that wishes I would not include it here. I apologize, Betty.

I will try to tell the story the right way, the way Drummer would want me to.)

*

She once had a clubfoot. There were thousands of clubfooted children in the mountains of Western North Carolina. A man named Seely, who was related by marriage to the famous guy E.W. Grove, would seek out these children and on his own time, at his own expense, he would get them the surgery they needed. Over time: thousands of surgeries at a cost of hundreds of thousands of dollars. They were Scottish hill people, many of them, and wouldn't let a doctor anywhere near. The man named Seely would risk his own safety to go up there, to tell them about the Shriner's hospital in Oxford, North Carolina, tell them they could trust the place because of the Masons trusting it. Mr. Seely saw to everything, and drove the children there and back in his own Willys Utility Truck, and checked on their recovery. He asked for nothing for himself.

As he was bringing one back home, her leg and ankle and foot wrapped in the cleanest white cloth she had ever seen, he firmly told her, "Stand up straight, child. Don't look away."

She never forgot.

Drummer.

August 6 – 12, 2004

My tent is my flush straight, my ace of pairs, chute coal, stop bus, station waiting, joint-strip, scene crime, casesuit, nest love, coat trench, pool swimming, pewchurch, paperfly, rug porch, my chair old-rocking, my stone grinding, my boardoakhead, box ice, stall donkey, holder candle, cupboard spice, wellstair, bucket bait, tunnel skunk, bell dinner, lick salt, blind deer, trap rabbit, markbench, linetide; my cairn river postmile, my deck-berth, my plot cemetery, my place known last. There, here, first converts easily to last, outside to inside-out, out-inside to inside, last there easily to first here.

High rainfall and still air and the shuffling-off heat of fauna and the emissions of flora bring the August and September blue-becoming-white haze and, underneath this, sounds trapped that normally would self-erase. The mummified wasps ranting inside spider webs, the passagio of birds during night migrations, the winged ants in sonorous clouds, and the silences rearranged by raccoons moving through high bracken in the thickets.

At the beginning of the week I had given them Hohner Blues Band C harps, in snap cases that Drummer had made and coated and baked and recoated and baked again into something resembling amber-soaked fabric. I had reminded each child that if she would hold the harmonica with only her thumb and first and second finger, the instrument would feel secure and she would not worry while she was beginning to breathe single notes.

I had helped them discover breathing in and out of the harp, only that much; with my own harp, I showed them how to breathe soft and then to breathe whisper-soft and then heavy and huffing-hard in order to produce melody from inside and at times far inside their bodies that wanted expression. We did not attempt a specific song, but already there was a country-lullaby quality in what Betty played and a three-little-birds-Bob-Marley-reggae phrase going on in Janet's playing.

Carla was supposed to join us on the last night of our August adventure. In the early morning Betty and Janet and I walked to the trailhead space where their mother's car should have been parked. We waited. In the early afternoon, I left them at the campsite and I hiked down again, but she had not come.

Back at the campsite, when I told them I was disappointed, although surprised because after all she had agreed to come, it was apparent that Betty and Janet already knew she would not appear.

"This — standing me up — does not seem fair," I said, receiving no response at all.

"Does this seem fair to you?" I asked.

I asked if they would like another lesson.

I explained that I would not yet permit anything but crisp single blow notes in tut-tut and too-too and do-woo-do-woo and koonkakoonk articulations. They must start and finish cleanly.

Hole 2, 3, 4, 5: I asked them to stay there, to blow — BLOW — blow — blow — DRAW — or blow-draw-blow-DRAW or draw-blow-DRAWAH-DRAWAH! to see what steam train arrived at or left that octave-station on the tracks of their breaths.

I had not taught harmonica to any of the other children on my sonic adventures. These two had asked.

I had once been an authoritative bioacoustician. I taught the sonic atavism and dispossession and dying effort of being fully alive. Needless to say, I wonder: Was I as absurd as I remember?

Purse your lips more when you *too-too*. Blow as if you are spitting a seed. Try to spit it farther. No double notes, please. Wet your lips with your tongue, Betty. Do not push your face out that way — bring the harp to your mouth. It's all right to look at the two-hole, which is your E note on the blow; and the three-hole is G and the four is C and the five is E again; and look again if you need to. And slide left to 1, which is C. Leave and forget to return, return and remember to leave.

"You have never spit a seed, have you?"

Janet looked at her sister who had slid left with sloppy gusto and who neither cared to be seen nor to see.

"You have not spit a seed or blown smoke or put on lipstick or probably wet your lips or ever kissed like you mean it," I said in my sergeant's voice, which was not quite Huge's voice, "and some day you may wish to execute a maneuver called a 'bee-jay.'

At that time you will expertly move up and down the octave in perfect control of your natural out-breath and your in-breath.

"And you will think fondly of Samantha Peabody's harmonica instruction."

Carla — I drew her to mind then — would have executed the BJ — inexpertly — for the sake of my husband who liked when I performed that maneuver, who quite sincerely felt it was inexhaustibly clever to say to me afterwards, "Play it again, Sam."

"Play what?" I would say, but then I would laugh. I laughed because I loved him so much that any redundant cleverness from him seemed — beyond my comprehension — nearly inexhaustibly clever.

I'd say, "Look, Robert, not *now*, I'm still wiping your grin off my face." He'd laugh, though I had used the exact punch line on him who knows how many hundreds of times. So much time has passed; I find myself thinking that he *probably* laughed.

Janet, transpersonally conscious of my thoughts as evident in the tone of my voice, asked me, "You spit a lot of seeds?"

"A lot of seeds," I said.

Our playing was receiving responses from the woods. Ground dwellers called back when they heard the softness of our round sounds, the "bouba-type" sounds of notes blown softly from the front of our mouths. Air dwellers called back when they heard the angular, spiky sounds, the "kiki-type" sounds of notes choked as we drew them down to our chests.

"Here," I said to them, "I want you to hear this: I am going to make the sounds of a train that has left a while ago but you can hear the shape you perceived, hear the last air-punching and steel-grinding sounds in clusters: long-draw-BLOW — draw-BLOW draw-long-BLOW. Do that with me."

We practiced together. Janet, percussively. Betty, reedily. We played only that much for three quarters of an hour before I sang and played the opening of "Shenandoah" for them and sang and played the corresponding clusters of sound in *"a-aWAY—you ROLLing-RI-IV-ER."* We agreed we would sing all the verses but would try to sing-say this part into the harmonica.

"War took it away," said Janet.

Betty answered — with no conviction — the question inside Janet: "Don't be scared."

I said, "When we play together we sound like a bagpipe with a hernia." I wanted to give them opportunity to leave the subject of Warren alone, to tell me only in the time and the way they would wish.

"He took her car away."

Betty said, "She can have her car back. He told her."

"He didn't. You never heard him — he didn't and she didn't and she doesn't know where he took it either."

"He drives her," Betty said. "Anywhere she wants to go."

Janet said, "Are you — what — are you —"

"I'm watching." Betty wiped the cover plates of her harp.

"He told me you were watching and he knew I was too and do you know what he said?

— he said — he said — what? — Betty, what did he say to *you*?"

Betty said, "I don't know," infuriating Janet.

I asked, "Is it your plan to talk as if I am not present?"

*

(That was your plan.)

*

Betty said, "He's back. Mom says he's back for good —"

"She did not! She —"

"—for good. We have to help him adjust. She says we lie about him and lied about him and we have to stop that, and we have to apologize so he knows we mean it."

Janet put her harp in the case. She snapped the case closed, gazed downward.

"You can talk with me," I said. "I am here with you. Have you heard?"

"I can?" Janet asked.

"No, not actually," I said. "I mean, the two of you — together — could talk with me." I could see that since moving back in with Carla, Warren had split the children, talking with each girl separately, manipulating them by never talking with either one in front of their graymother. I could see that Carla, perhaps only by accident, had split them as well, deciding some information could be told to Betty but not to Janet, some information could be explained differently to Janet than to Betty.

I said, "If you talk with me, I will listen."

"He put a bug on you," Janet said. "Did you get it off?"

I asked, "Are you going to talk with me?"

"He *did not*," said Betty. "He put the bug on *you*."

I hesitated to believe: he had bugged them, and he told them he had bugged them — or he had simply told each one in a frightening way that he had placed an insect on her.

"Did you tell your mother about the bug?" I asked.

"Hmm?" said Betty.

"I couldn't find it," said Janet.

"Me neither," said Betty. "He's a liar. He makes it so you can't tell and so she can't tell."

I asked them to take me back a few steps, back further than the bugs.

They explained that at the end of July their mother had taken an entire weekend off to spend with them, that she'd told them of how she "made peace" with Warren, and how good it felt to be forgiven by him. She'd told them there was nothing better than forgiveness, and they would see how you could have mercy if you could have forgiveness, you could have justice if you could have mercy.

She had forgiven him everything, she told them.

I was certain this was true. I did not believe this was a ploy on Carla's part. Instead of bringing him into her home in a spider net, she had invited him there to set his own traplines, which would vibrate to signal him about new information he had captured.

*

We took our harps out of the cases. We repeatedly played one phrase.

*

"Could be worse," I said. Our playing quieted the world around our campsite. I mean to say that all of the responses from the woods seemed to me to be the quieter not-knowing sounds. *'cross the WI-IDE Mis-SOUR-eeee*, we played.

Janet said, "I'm not even tired."

'cross the WI-IDE Mis-SOOR-eeee.

"Your glasses are crooked," said Betty.

Your glasses! I thought, your damn glasses!

I said, "We should clean them more often. You should let me clean them for you. Okay?"

"They're dirty?" asked Betty.

"Let me see." I cleaned the lenses of Betty's glasses. I had to use my pocketknife because the tiny, realistic copper sunflowers were glued onto the stems: I dug out the perfect bug and back-up bug.

"Mine?" asked Janet.

I dug the same devices from Janet's. "Awful," I said.

I held the tiny metal flowers out in my palm. This was the kind of cheap equipment that would limit Warren's monitoring to only the conversations in their graymother's home.

"Will it be all right for me to keep them?" I asked.

❧

(You know now, of course, that what I held were listening devices, but you really could not understand then, and even if you had understood, that kind of evil would have been too incomprehensible for you to accept as truth.

You were only children, after all.)

❧

We crossed the wide Missouri. Again and again, we crossed. I talked to them about the acoustic energy of Scottish Highlander pipes. I explained infrasonic energy, and though I offered a clear description of how such sound makes us more like insect-hearers than human-hearers in the ways it alters our experiences of qualitative time and in the ways it decides our waking and sleeping paths in dreamtime and dreamspace, I felt I'd failed. If one had no understanding whatsoever of teaching, one could say Samantha Peabody was once a teacher. If one had no understanding of mothering, one could say Samantha Peabody mothered those two children on their sonic adventures.

We bundled inside the tent and then outside again where we could walk in the new moon starlight and could locate track paths of various human and animal kinds. The sunlight at certain hours will help, the moonlight will help, but strong starlight uniquely reveals the substrate. The sound of a hungry shrew — twewee ... ree! — its broken-refrigerator-door-opening-and-closing squeakings — gave us the opportunity to find the shrew's track paths. They overlapped with deeper stippled scars and underscarrings that we deductively guessed were there from the Backstreet Boys intensively dancing, and that we inductively theorized were there from the stampeding of hoofed animals in violent recent storms and storms from earlier years and even from earlier centuries.

The pond was our destination since there are many forms of track paths to and from a pond. Approximately 3.5 meters from the edge of the pond, we lowered ourselves to our knees and onto our stomachs.

There was a rustling near us.

Quietly, quietly, I asked them if it could be a woodchuck, but they answered that it might not be near us at all. From a distance of seventy miles the metal and concrete drum-sound of cities could come into our woods as a deep, low frequency; in the cool air of night the delocalized city voices could sink into the forest bed where all of the sonic machinings would manifest as worm-bizzlings. Betty *heard*. Janet *heard*. In eleven months, they had learned to hear.

Janet located a track path to and from the pond that she said she knew by heart. She pointed to a faint trace illustrating the dragging-dancing step of some four-legged synesthete.

I asked if she remembered the teenage porcupine's name, which fairly insulted her.

✻

(It is possible that you still remember: QweT-Tek-KET Kwook-kkkwoTTee.)

✻

"Look at this," Janet said. When she brushed her hand over the patch of gold on the path, gnats swarmed a thousandfold onto her neck, blind-searched her face, disappeared into her hair and then into the air. This happened in half of one second.

We lay on our sides, defining a niche in which we could look at each other's faces and listen. I said, "I'm kind of sorry you heard all of that in July. I'm displeased that I did not control the situation with more precision. Your mother and Elaine — they were unloading a whole lot." I had felt the old burdens and the new hurt with such focus on myself that I had allowed collateral damage to Betty and Janet. "I mean I am kind of sorry. You needed to hear some of that horseshit because you are not always here in my woods where I can care for you." You are in his trap for you that is baited with your graymother, I thought; and I thought, You are in his trap for her that is baited with you.

I said, "You need to put together what is possible for you, and you need the materials to do that." And, I thought, How terrible that the materials you hold are what remains after the draggings and gashings and stampedings of adults running from and ripping apart each other, and carrying whatever is left somewhere to hide the bones from view.

"I don't know why I spoke with you as I did about effing. I — listen, please — I'm a horny thing and rotting and I should not have used the f-word, your mother was right about that and right to be angry with me, and I have not exactly wanted to take all of that back, which does not speak well of me, and I want to apologize to you both, but no words are coming for the apology though the proper time is here, and there will not be many more opportunities."

Betty closed her eyes. She put her hands over her ears.

"Will you accept my apology?"

Betty, not accepting my apology, which she heard perfectly well through her hands, gazed weirdly at me.

Janet, not accepting my apology, said, "We can't do anything," and she asked, "Can we?" and she listened, really listened in order to know if I would say something that would help her feel less fear. "Do you know something?"

Did I? Did I know anything at all? Was I so intent on retreating from the world that I would leave her and Betty behind?

Betty had unriddled what Janet was going to say next. She pleaded with Janet: "Don't."

I learned then that Mrs. Preibus had returned, that a heavy cabinet safe had come with her, that Mrs. Preibus disclosed the full contents of the gun cabinet to Carla, that Mrs. Preibus changed all the house's locks. Their mother had no keys, and no land- or cell-line. She had no law practice, no link to family or friends. She went to the grocery store with Mrs. Preibus. She took her children to school and picked them up with Mrs. Preibus as her driver.

I said, "The situation is beyond our control."

Betty said, "But you —"

I am the cowardly witness to the abuse of my only daughters, I am the murderer of the man I loved, I am self-delivered to the hell inside the sole heaven — these woods — in which I believe.

*

I remember how in July Carla had scratched at my tent at three or four in the morning.

"Sam," she had said, and not softly.

"Bitch," I said.

"Are they okay in there? Are they asleep?"

"Bitch," I said. The word "bitch" has a spiky yet round sound-shape: I heard my hatred for her in the word, and I heard my love for her. A conversion is possible in a single word.

I said, "Go back to your tent, bitch."

"Elaine's driving me crazy."

She laughed when I said, "Tell me about it."

All night, Elaine had been sleeping deeply but talking in her sleep. She was still spewing words, spewing some more, sleeping, saying, maybe it was in her dreams she was saying: "Couldn't —" Betty and Janet had been hard asleep, ears closed.

Carla would not leave. "I can't bear you," I said. "How can I bear you?"

That is what she needed: for me to bear her. She spilled out that Robert was one in a set of games for her, that the adoption of the children was supposed to put at risk all of her decades of game playing, but the strategy had not worked. At the time she took on Robert she had wanted to escalate the risks, to know that she had more at stake and to bet her law practice, which she hated by then, on a bad hand. The Judge was a new level of game playing, and she had made their arrangement public in order to inspire jealousy, since every lawyer wanted to have a judge in the bag and to take him out and milk his venom and ingest it for the sake of being fully inoculated.

"I wasn't sure about what I felt for Robert," she had said. "Until after the divorce weakened him. I guess I weakened with him. So. For a few hours we thought we loved each other but then knew better a few hours later. Over and over. I told him all of the divorce terms were your ideas."

"You bitch," I said.

"He didn't doubt me. I'm saying this as a fact. I'm not saying this to be mean. He believed you would do all of that — and all the way to the outer limits — to him."

"Does any of that matter?" I asked her. I thought, Tell me how that matters.

"Let me come in. I won't talk any more. It's good to have this out — I've been saying these things inside me for many years, and some of them I've said for *fifty* years. And now I've said them. I'm tired. I want to be in there with you and my children, the four of us. Let me come in, Sam."

I thought, Tell me how any of that matters if we have Janet and Betty in our lives and can love them and feel how we are loved by them?

"Sam?"

"Go away. You *bitch*."

※

Janet definitively identified the porcupine track path. She remembered the question she had been asked there: "Did you kiss me?" I could easily perceive that she remembered, since remembered pleasure and pain had not submerged too deeply in her.

Is Mr. Kwook-kkkwoTTee near? I did not have to ask the question aloud, she heard me thinking my asking.

"There's something else," she said.

I sensed that Drummer might be nearby in the woods. She has never confirmed it for me, but I believe Drummer stayed near us during the summer hours that Carla and Elaine visited.

"What is that sound?" I asked.

I was certain she knew. Janet could hear so keenly.

※

(Janet, did you know the person in the woods was your gray-mother, having none of Drummer's skill as a wraith, hiding near us, probably completely prone and miserable on the cold forest floor, trying to decide if she would come out from hiding, having no idea why she was there but not yet coming out of hiding?

My own hearing, taking in microsonic details beyond your apprehension, did not give me a clear answer about whether Carla was there.

I think you — both of you — must have known.)

*

Janet said, loud enough to be heard well beyond our campsite, "Why would she do it?" and meant why would Carla, a person with so much power in the world, relent her power to Warren in her own home; and meant why would she have hurt Samantha Peabody and still have felt it was all right to bring her children to the enemy's lair; and meant why would she have injured her youngest daughter, and why that one time only, because Janet had taken Carla's gift from Robert, the black scarf; and why not strike Janet again and again with no reason, and why not again with reason enough once Janet defied her commands regarding Warren and Mrs. Preibus; and why had her mother not forgiven herself for injuring Janet and not forgiven herself for betraying Samantha and not forgiven herself for being involved with Warren, and then, insanely, insanely, insanely, forgiven Warren for all he had done?

"If that is you, Drummer, go home," I said into the air. "If that is you, Carla — Carla, is that you? — come home."

Betty said, "Please. Please, Mom." She had no voice at all. I might have only imagined that Betty spoke.

September 3 – 9, 2004

For over forty years the red spruce and the Fraser fir have gone in a shambling-down and stress-cracking and shattering-apart dying. In the places here where no visible evidence of them remains, the soil breathes out the vinegar-stink of high acid levels. But the ash trees hold. And the maples send out their whirling, murmuring samaras.

My mother, in love with trees and having no apparent curiosity about them, had taped a handwritten note onto her sewing table: *"I like trees because they seem more resigned to the way they have to live than other things do."* The note was there even when I was a toddler, and I thought she had written the words. Something about that assumption made sense since the sewing table was a distinctive dark-stained pine. I liked that she had written the words down, but years later I liked even more that she had brought the inexpensive cloth of them to her singing workplace from the author's singing workplace; she had copied down the passage from Willa Cather's *O Pioneers!*

It was the first Thursday in September. I knew this would be my last week with Janet and Betty, and I was trying to push them from my thoughts.

*

(Not once, not a single time since October 2003, have I succeeded in pushing you from my thoughts.)

*

Staring up into the seed-shedding maples, I called to mind Huge, who, amazed by the rapidity of his own decline, told me he was happy his form of lung cancer would pull him down fast and not, as he said, "in endless, boring turnarounds." A few days before the end, Biz, without giving Huge advance notice, offered me one of his harmonica cases, felt-lined spaces for seven major keys, the hinged wooden cover painted black. He'd given her the affectionate nickname "Biz" for her habits of "being all up in my business."

On the front of the case he had glued a worse-for-wear playing card, a Jack of Hearts.

After seven years of once-a-week lessons, Huge, who offered me friendship more pure than any I had ever reached for or been offered, was plainly sad about my playing. "You have ruined my day so goddamn many times," he said in the way an honest friend can finally speak his mind — and, on the bend of that damn-note, his heart.

*

Elaine brought Betty and Janet to me at the trailhead parking lot. She explained that Carla had asked her to bring them and pick them up. Carla and Warren's instructions were firm: they were allowed one day and night with me. The sonic adventure was over. They would not be permitted to come to me ever again.

What could I say to these, my two children, my own, my lost things? I held out my arms.

"Ka-ching!" said Janet.

"Ka-ching!" said Betty.

I told them everything was chill. I asked if they had their green gloves and their green socks. I asked if they had their down vests and black cotton pants.

They were wearing their boots. "I am glad to see your feet," I said, "and your boots on your feet, and your creeping socks!" And did they bring books? None? Supplies for Samantha Peabody? Their harps? They crushed themselves against me, not letting go. I said, "Oh, Betty, oh, Janet! I am so grateful for the return of my reliable sources of obscene wealth!"

We laughed together, we did, and why would we have not? For at least eight thousand years, the ice flowing inside humans has gathered the earth's broken pieces into it, and that flow moves counter to the flow of the pure-blue, pure-clear ice of us; the glacial scouring sound is something like the ensonifying laughter of my daughters Janet and Betty.

We sent Elaine away.

*

(I have wondered: why would Elaine, her long relationship with Carla destroyed, agree to help her bring you and me together for that one last day and night? My theory is that Elaine's love is the fearless kind that leads to mercy. Her love is not like mine, so fearful and so merciless.)

*

We walked the trail to our camp, stopping often to listen to the oar tips of sounds for which we could not find the complete oars. One could say we were composing the echoings and settlings. As I had taught them, they were trying to be patient in moving their hearing beyond the categorizing impulse. I worried that they were remembering stratas of sound they had previously encountered at these trail sections, which would have meant that they were projecting the appearance of those sounds upon the dimension of the present moment. I pre-corrected them for that bad habit: "If you think you hear what you heard then, what you actually hear now will be hid."

Very quietly, Janet said, "Duh." I was pleased to observe moisture on her glasses, since that closing of the visual field refreshes hearing. Her glasses were much too large for her small triangular-type face.

I placed their heads against each side of my chest — we were still walking and we did not at all break stride — and I breathed onto the lenses of their glasses in order to absolutely obscure the visual field. "There," I said.

The largest trees grumbled like torqued mainmasts, and in the next instant they sent absorbed shock waves downward and upward. The tallest of them, a white pine of over 60 meters, offered such an impressive report of the thunder that Betty and Janet could walk to that exact one. They nodded at me and each nodded also at the white pine. Tree and child made themselves understood: *perfect transmission.*

I did not ask if they might ever understand why I would not stay with them after the events in August, would not enter the fires they had entered. They knew that when I left my camp and went into Asheville with them I had every intention to protect them.

⁂

(Did you know? I believe you knew.)

⁂

I was left helpless by their mother's vociferous objections to bringing any charges against Warren.

Helpless.

In August after the incident — I am getting to the incident soon — Betty and Janet asked me to protect them from Warren and, implicitly, from Carla.

With Park Ranger Ruck's help I had been able to get Betty and Janet to Elaine's home in Asheville where Elaine and Tim and Amelia guarded them for three days, after which police officers arrested and briefly jailed all three adults, and "recovered" the children. When Elaine and Tim and Amelia appealed to legal counsel to guide them, they learned a great deal about Judge Warren's power and about the terrifyingly threatening power of that legal team of Warren and Carla. A year later Elaine and Tim and Amelia were still under investigation for child endangerment. Two and three and four years later the unrelenting investigations of them proceeded to the attorney general's office. All of Elaine's savings were completely drained as a result of the legal expenses she assumed for her and Tim and Amelia. The intimidated local and state media reported only enough of "the crime" to permanently smear three good people's reputations; no single word was published about the accountability of Warren who was, at that time, a sitting judge.

＊

(None of this has ever been rightly explained to you.

And to explain now is to rescue facts that have repeatedly melted and changed form and flooded. They are already flowing toward you.)

＊

At our food site, we ate crackers and turkey jerky.

"You will miss the daily feed," I said.

"No, Pea, we will not," said Janet.

"Not by any measurement," said Betty.

Before entering our tent, we conscientiously groomed each other. "In less than fifteen minutes it will be naptime," I said.

We shared creek water freshly purified. Their throats, instruments altered by physiological development, made sounds different than they had made months earlier. In my August 2004 notebook citation I had written: "Betty/Janet channels conducive to greater number of stable vocalizations — illustration: 'Shenandoah.'"

Betty and Janet encased me.

We crossed the wide Missouri.

"Is your mother —"

"She's with Warren. And Mrs. Preibus," said Betty.

I was glad that Elaine was not hovering near, talking with herself as if able to really ever listen to her own voice. She has written to offer me help. She asked me to help her through her second divorce in 2011, through her 2013 diabetes scare, through approximately four years she has called her "space-suit time" in the vacuum of her solitary and impoverished mid-eighties. During these past twelve years, I have had contact with her only through letters. Not once have I gone to her when she has needed me.

※

(In May I had encouraged Park Ranger Ruck to share Gooser with Elaine. I have learned that they are an exuberant threesome. They live together — Ellenby Ruck's apartment on Laurentide Street, Oteen, NC — phone book number under her name.

They would enjoy a visit from you. You would find Gooser's and Ellenby Ruck's company tolerable.

Not knowing you really at all, Elaine loves you two. Tim and Amelia write to me; they ask about you.

Drummer asks about you. She wishes she had absconded with and hidden you; and made you build her an outhouse with a heating and cooling system; and let her arrange your marriages to Ricky and Chad — who are respectable citizens and, by the way, available bachelors — and given you four the run of the place, and taught you to raise black hens and white gamecocks and to master the operations of her little still; and made you the own-born cousin kin of Silvershawl so that you could be mists in these mountains, and rouse and rest upon and lift from and slip off their old shoulders like ghost-blankets.

I will not here employ the f-word, but I will acknowledge that Drummer tells me her thoughts about you on my March and September stoned-wild-demon-wrestling near-death sublime f-fests with her. I believe you understand.)

*

Their embouchures were tense and in need of some loosening and softening at the front of their mouths. Betty's Carter-Family-type intonations and Janet's spliffy hitch-beats needed improvement. I hoped they would practice, improve.

We crossed the river again. Nodding off, they handed me their harps and cases.

*

(I am certain you recollect little of it. Since your mother has lived all of this time — twelve years — with Warren acting as a kind of prison warden. Since Mrs. Preibus has been your second mother and your graymother's personal prison guard. Since you have freed yourselves.

Elaine has told me you sometimes visit Carla and Warren and Mrs. Preibus, and that you look after their care in every way you can.

I shall quote one of your letters, received 3-3-12: "WTF?"

WTF. WTF. But how is your decision to be in the world — all the way in and accepting the life-stealing punishments and sufferings and the thresholds of life-giving awe there at the world's precipices — how are those decisions less eccentric choices than my own so-called eccentric choices?

What do you offer Carla and Warren and Mrs. Preibus?

From almost any angle your choice looks like Stockholm Syndrome; by definition it is "abnormal." I know you love Carla, and you understand she loves you yet cannot help you because she is lost. In order to hear her thundering heart, you must plunge your heads in and have your breaths taken away, and hear what you hear.)

*

After their nap, we hiked to The Black Tongue. Through the trees came the sound of brick smacking brick: mature white-tailed bucks. We held still, and were rewarded by hearing the sniffing and grunting of a buck holding in the scent of a doe, and sounding and re-sounding the scent against the roof of his mouth.

I once more showed Betty and Janet the pillow-and-cradle formation. We stayed there until dusk, the sky lowering quietness over us, pressing the quiet down. We looked for and found pungent scrapes made by bucks, and we found antler velvet rubbed on trees and bushes nearby.

I did not tell them then what exactly had happened. I have pieced the story together with the help of Drummer and Ranger Ruck and Case Curran.

*

(Case said for me to tell you, "Hi there, you little bitches.")

*

Case had been setting traps at various small-animal-track traces near the gorge. He was, as ever, incompetent at poaching. He did a poor job of baiting the traps and of hiding his work under dirt and damp chestnut leaves and under the pine needles he cured a certain way before hauling them there in a cloth sack.

He thought — he actually believed this — that on certain dates the rangers took nights off. He did not know Park Ranger Ruck, that much is clear. She had no hope Case would ever do any of his work legally, so she was monitoring him while she was also thinking she wished he had at least been properly taught how to trap, even how to use the proper traps. He finished, and, with a remaining trap in hand, headed to a coppice near our camp.

*

I go to this place on new moon nights like tonight. I feel the woods are darker there, that I am darkened there where colder starlight judders in the coppice.

*

Near a system of root knots in that area Case liked to hunt ginseng. He planted ginseng there also, pushing seeds beneath leaf litter in a four-hundred-fifty-square-foot area he had been cultivating — illegally — for over a decade. He was seng-ing when he saw Warren stalking Carla, who was huddled on the ground near the place that Betty and Janet and I had once heard bear cubs.

Carla was there to run from Warren. Or she was there to run to us.

I suppose she had stolen a car, though maybe she had somehow stolen her own car: it is not possible to know, is it? Perhaps

Elaine knows. If Elaine knows, needless to say, I will eventually learn the answer.

This is my version of what happened. I didn't tell it then.

I'm telling it now. I wish to tell it accurately. I wish to tell it incautiously.

Warren felt a large animal pounce upon him, roll him onto his back, rip the hair from above his temples as if trying to peel back his scalp. He felt his solar plexus struck viciously. The lithe creature, with tremendous power in its forelegs and hind legs, turned Warren onto his stomach and cracked his back ribs with its hard skull, and then flipped him and flipped him in order to repeat the attack, which was done with such unimaginable speed that Warren might have been hit twenty times, or thirty.

Warren felt the creature's wet paws push a clod of dirt or a clump of dung — or a pine cone — past his teeth and deep into his throat; for a moment he was certain the creature had pushed its tongue there, far down into him where it could taste Warren's bile.

He felt jaws closing over and puncturing his face with pressure so great that the force almost made his eyes give way from his eyesockets. His nose spewed blood, which only further enraged the creature, which wiped its slaked maw against his lower back and buttocks and thighs, and horned at him with its muzzle.

And then Warren was dragged away by his ankles. He was slapped against tree trunks and ripped across sharp fins of rock and fists of roots in order to tenderize but not break him.

The nightmare creature, Case Curran, took him to the edge of the gorge.

Park Ranger Ruck watched all of this. Drummer, who had heard the disturbance, watched the last part of the attack. I, in my daydreams, elaborate upon the story in order to take satisfaction in the beginning, middle, and end.

Drummer and Ruck were not surprised by Case's strength, but his rage stunned them. He whipped the belt from Warren's pants, and bound his legs together, drawing his ankles and feet toward his face so that Warren looked like a scorpion attacking itself. He pulled Warren's hands and arms to a point of extreme tension above his head, and he roped them in a furious hurry but with precision.

Case removed his big double-spring trap from Warren's face. He pushed another clot into his throat, a gruel made from Warren's own teeth and the hair torn from his head. This caused desperate heaving.

He wiped Warren's face, pulling open his closed, swollen eyes.

He lifted him over his head and held him there, a man three times Case's weight. At the moment he made eye contact, he threw Warren off the edge of the gorge.

When Drummer and Ruck approached Case, he came to them, his head low, his shoulders and his whole upper body hunched. "Like a sorrowing lamb" was how Drummer described him to me.

"You saw thet?" Case said. His forehead was bruised, bloody.

"We did," said Ellenby.

"Kicks in," he said. "Scares me to death."

"Yes," Ellenby said, "that is scary. I know."

"He was goin' to kill her. I smelled thet on him."

"What *are* you?" she asked.

He could not answer. One can be asked that question many times through the years and not know the answer.

The three of them made a four-hour hike down to find Warren. He was alive.

They were pleased that he could walk, that Case had not broken Warren's legs and knees and ankles. Warren had, in fact, been expertly "packaged" by Case as if for gutting and skinning and keeping the pelt unmarred.

They untied and ungagged him, put him on his swollen feet, pushed him forward.

This I find intriguing: afterwards, Warren did not remember being tied, gagged, untied, ungagged. He did not remember groaning with every painful step. He did not remember being treated roughly by Drummer and Ranger Ruck and Case when he staggered or stopped in order to rest. He did remember staring into animal-wild eyes before his nightmare plunge.

Seven hours later, they hiked out with the large shitbag of hurt. Ranger Ruck transported him to the hospital.

That is most of the story.

Weeks later, Warren requested that the Pisgah Forest Service euthanize the bear that had attacked him. He worried that others might be in danger, that is what he said. He demanded the bear's hide and skull. He was told he was attacked by an elderly female bear known to the mountain folks there as Ruby. He was not shown their file photo of the taxidermied bear posed standing, arms open, behind the Stanley's~~Acker's~~Stanley's bar in Cord. Ruby appeared ready to serve drinks. She was no larger than he.

That is most of the story. And, I wonder, do I have this part right: Carla, an apparition, strode into our camp. When Betty and Janet and I greeted her, she turned away.

She turned away. She said, "Get off me."

Her sole concern was for Warren.

*

Our last day and night together had passed.

I wanted them to know how to find Drummer whenever they needed to be lost with her. If they wished to have news of me, she could provide that in person. If they wanted to hear the trace-sounds of me, I could be heard there at Drummer's.

In the evening, Janet and Betty and I walked all the way back to the trailhead. From the trailhead, we followed my hand-drawn map to Drummer's home, which was completely obscured in evening mist. With the concentration of sparks hungering for dry groundcover, the children gazed at the place where the cabin should stand. I said, "You know how to find Drummer?" "Got it," said Betty.

"Got it," said Janet.

October 17, 2016

I hear white-throated sparrows, transients, moving on.

Janet turns nineteen today. I turn eighty.

I hear, from far above, the sound of a hawk at great height and straining to go higher. I hear, from a small apple orchard along a streambed that could be nearly ten miles away, a flock of grackles at maximum shrieking obnoxiousness, and the blistering reactions of the blue jays near them, and the responses of the four-legged creatures intimidated by the blue jays. I hear gnats slurring in vortical swarms. With arising inflected note and a note soft-falling, the catbirds: I can hear them if I will hear only them and will not allow myself to remember hearing them at other times, and will not look at them.

I will hear them if I will not ruin the transmission by welcoming in my other senses.

The sounds coming to visit me would be lost in the moment I opened my eyes and my arms, and smelled and tasted and touched educing fragrance and sweetness and chill.

And if I will not imagine what I hear but will actually hear, then what comes to me are broom-sweep sounds, the wings of the nuthatches, the thrushes, bluebirds, purple finches, sparrows flying through and impossibly, impossibly, audibly plucking but not breaking the acrobat-threads of balloon spiders riding the wind, letting the threads go, extending their legs before parachuting on the air currents, and re-launching.

Distant, faint thunder is inside the sunlight today. Sleet striking a pond at a higher elevation vibrates inside the sunlight today, and the vocalizations of creatures at the entrance to their burrows. One might believe that today the sun has touched the faces of them, has brushed the charged roots and branches and treetops and the glistening webs and feathers and fur in order to sing and to be heard.

Author's Note

October 17, 2016, marked the centennial anniversary of the day President Woodrow Wilson proclaimed the Pisgah National Forest as the first eastern national forest.

In the Pink Beds area of the Pisgah, Dr. Carl Alwin Schenck established the Biltmore Forest School. This first school in forestry management in the United States resulted in the Pisgah being named "The Cradle of Forestry." Dr. Schenck received the unflagging patronage of the Vanderbilt family for this visionary effort to defend logging-scarred forests from irrecoverable devastation and to preserve for common people what President Theodore Roosevelt called our "citizen's share" of the "rumpled, roadless quilt of original America."

Three forest districts, the Pisgah Ranger District, the Grandfather Ranger District, and the Appalachian Ranger District, comprise the Pisgah National Forest. *At the Gate of All Wonder* is set in the Pisgah Ranger District. The author, attempting to be loyal to the dreamlike elements of his novel, has fictionalized the locations and names of trails, creeks, campgrounds, landmarks, peaks, and other formations. In an effort to be respectful of nature's own creations, the author has honored the factual soundscape of the Pisgah in its changing seasons.

At this historic moment for celebration of American forestry, The Wilderness Society and the Western North Carolina Alliance are in a struggle to preserve the Nantahala-Pisgah. According to Josh Kelly, a public lands field biologist with WNCA, "Timber harvests for the last twelve years have been sustainable, averaging less than 800 acres annually, and there is an opportunity to increase that number while doing ecologically beneficial work. Yet the divisions of the 'timber wars' of the '80s and '90s still persist," and a "push for more logging has been accompanied by hostility toward protecting old-growth forests, natural heritage areas, and backcountry areas."

If you would like to support preservation of the Pisgah Ranger District, please call (828) 877–3265 or visit www.fs.usda.gov/nfsnc.

Acknowledgments

Excerpts from this novel appeared in *Shadowgraph Two* (Summer 2014).

I'm grateful that you have listened and have heard: Chris Hale, Tony Hoagland, Miriam Altshuler, Don Mercer, Bob and Tina Hvitfeldt, Nancy J. Allen, Kent Jacobs, Sallie Ritter, Jeffrey Levine, Jim Schley, Kristina Marie Darling, Marie Gauthier, Sebastian Matthews, Emilie White, Rachel Haley Himmelheber, Andrea Barrett, Joan Silber, Karen Brennan, Berni Smyth, Peter Turchi, Reed Turchi, Robert Boswell, Ellen Bryant Voigt, Rick Russo, Sarah Stone, Heather McHugh, Peg Alford Pursell, Cass Pursell, Rich Yanez, Todd McKinney, Erin Stalcup, Justin Robert Lightfoot Bigos, Rus Bradburd, Don Kurtz, Margaret Susan Bonham, Mary Wolf, Lou Ocepek, Paula Moore, Evan Lavender-Smith, Dave Rutschman, Joe Scapellato, Lynette D'Amico, Sally Ball, Matthea Harvey, Laura Kasischke, Martha Rhodes, Dale Neal, Rhonda Steele, Philip Bernick, and through many years, Chris Burnham. The rangers at the Pisgah National Forest Ranger District welcomed my questions, the simplest and the most complex. All of you who have adventured with me during my forty years of teaching, thank you for the moments when we have lost the worn paths and have wandered.

Other Books from Tupelo Press

See our complete list at www.tupelopress.org